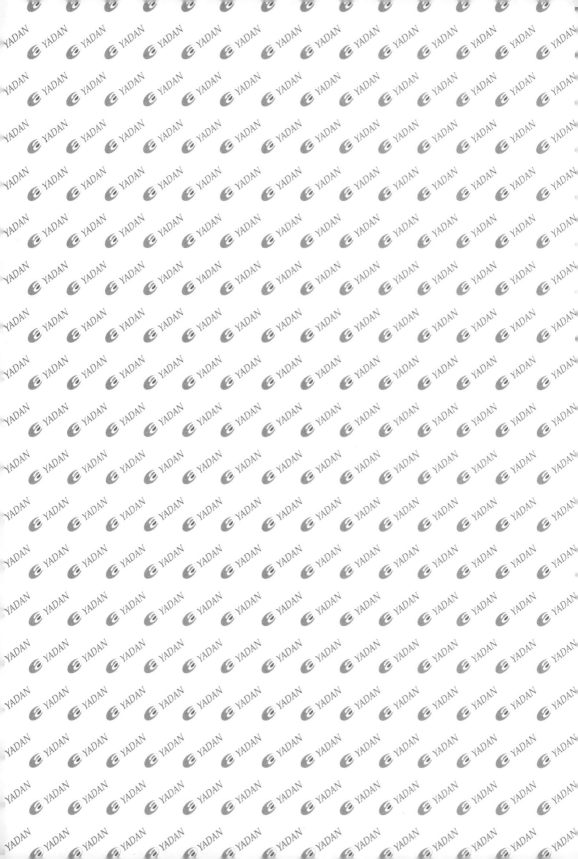

+ MP3

準備GEPT Pro企業英檢的必備工具書

完全掌握企業英檢的命題方向和題型
不但能幫您高分過關，英語實力也隨之大增

史上最強

張文娟 著

GEPT Pro

企業英檢
一本就夠

Mastering the GEPT Pro
The General English Proficiency Test
Professional

本書專為想要參加企業英檢的學習者編撰的

隨書所附的CD亦為最佳英語自學教材，平時多聽，善加模仿，成效驚人。

● 企業英檢的完整資訊：
提供所有關於企業英檢(GEPT Pro)
必知的Q&A。

● 企業英檢的準備要點：
就企業英檢要測驗的聽力和閱讀兩大
項目，提綱挈領，針對各類題型一一
提供對策。

● 企業英檢的模擬試題：
提供仿真模擬試題兩回，並附上中文
詳盡翻譯與解析。

● 企業英檢的必背420字：
提供出現頻率最高的420個單字，加上
同義字，不但為企業英檢的常考單字，
也是工作場合常用到的單字。

目 - Contents - 錄

005　第一章 🌐 關於GEPT Pro「企業英檢」的問與答

009　第二章 🌐 聽力講座

035　第三章 🌐 閱讀講座

067　第四章 🌐 第一回模擬試題
113----------第一回模擬試題中文翻譯與解答

157　第五章 🌐 第二回模擬試題
199----------第二回模擬試題中文翻譯與解答

239　第六章 🌐 必背420字

Chapter. 01

關於 GEPT Pro
「企業英檢」的問與答

astering the GEPT Pro
e General English Proficiency Test
Professional

史上最強
GEPT Pro
企業英檢一本就夠

Q：什麼是GEPT Pro 「企業英檢」？

A：GEPT Pro 「企業英檢」是專門為國人所設計的商業職場英語能力測驗，相較於一般英語能力檢定，較偏重於職場英語，而其內容特色著重於台灣的企業情境。

Q：誰會需要考GEPT Pro 「企業英檢」？

A：無論是於外商工作或於本土公司扮演對外窗口的員工，都可藉由GEPT Pro 「企業英檢」的檢定結果來展現個人英語職能；而想要獲得上述英語相關工作的求職者，無論是已畢業者或尚在求學的學生，都可以將此測驗作為學習目標來提昇商業英語能力，將英語溝通力化為職場利器。

Q：GEPT Pro 「企業英檢」的測驗內容為何？

A：測驗內容範圍包括國際金融、國際貿易、外匯交易、投資、保險、行銷及企業管理等領域，試題情境包含客戶洽談、商務會議、財經新聞報導、專題演講、商務電子郵件、業務提案與報告、市場資訊、商業管理期刊、網站資訊等等。

Q：GEPT Pro 「企業英檢」的測驗方式與評分方式為何？

A：「企業英檢」一次測驗同時檢定「實用級」與「專業級」兩個級數，包含聽力與閱讀測驗兩個項目，而其聽力與閱讀測驗為紙筆測驗，共70題，測驗時間約1.5小時。

◆ 測驗方式：

聽力	第一部份：簡短對話與談話	選擇	15題	約35分鐘
	第二部份：談話	配合	10題	
	第三部份：長篇談話與對話	選擇	10題	
閱讀	第一部份：圖表、書信、短文	選擇	17題	60分鐘
	第二部份：長篇文章	配合	18題	

計分方式：本測驗滿分120分，聽力佔40%（滿分48分）、閱讀佔60%（滿分72分）。

◆ 分級：

專業級	總分達90分。（相當於全民英檢中高級）
實用級	總分60~89分，且聽力成績不低於14分，閱讀成績不低於21分。（相當於全民英檢中級）

◆企業英檢能力說明：

企業英檢分級	能力說明	
專業級 總分達90分	聽力	能聽懂 ●同業、客戶洽談 ●業務會議談話、業務提案報告 ●商管領域相關的討論 ●財經新聞 ●商管領域相關的專業演講
	閱讀	能閱讀 ●商管領域相關的期刊 ●商管領域相關的市場資訊 ●商管領域相關的文件 ●商管領域相關的長篇文章
實用級 總分達60分，且聽力 成績不低於14分，閱 讀成績不低於21分	聽力	能大致聽懂 ●工作場所的電話留言及一般對話 ●商管領域相關的簡報、產品介紹 ●商管領域相關的新聞報導 ●商管領域相關的訪談

Chapter. 02
聽力講座

Mastering the GEPT Pro
The General English Proficiency Test
Professional

史上最強
GEPT Pro
企業英檢一本就夠

1. 聽力重點：

◎先掃讀問題以快速判斷出可能的場景和情節。

◎於播放對話或談話時尋找關鍵字：5W & how：
Who、What、Where、When、Why
How (How much, How long, How often, How about)

◎常考：時間（包括日期）和金錢的數字。

◎在仔細聆聽的過程中，若聽到陌生單字、片語，不要因此而慌亂或停頓，先依情境猜測意思，繼續冷靜聽完全部內容。

◎因為企業英檢答錯不倒扣分數，所以若不知正確答案，也應隨意選個答案，不要不答。

2. 常見的格式與內容：

◎Short conversation　簡短對話
範例：
(Telephone conversation)

W: May I have your name and date of birth?

M: Yes, my name is Wang, Datong, and my date of birth is March 11, 1987.

W: Yes, that's correct. What can I do for you?

M: My credit card is stolen. Could you please check if somebody has taken money out using the card?

W: Sure. Let's see⋯So far there hasn't been such a case. Would you want me to block the card for you?

W: Of course. Thank you very much.

中文翻譯:

(電話對話)

女:可以告訴我您的姓名和生日嗎?

男:可以,我叫王大同,我的生日是1987年3月11日。

女:好,完全正確。有什麼需要我為您服務的嗎?

男:我的信用卡被偷了。您能幫我查一下是否有人盜刷嗎?

女:沒問題。讓我看看⋯⋯到目前為止沒有。您需要我為信用卡辦理止付嗎?

男:當然。謝謝您。

Question 1: Why is the man making this phone call?

A. He has run out of money.

B. He wants to take a loan.

C. His credit card is lost.

D. He wants to double-check his bill.

問題1：這男子為什麼打這通電話？
A. 他的錢用光了。
B. 他想要辦理貸款。
C. 他的信用卡被偷了。
D. 他想要核對他的帳單。

答案：C
本題在測驗對話內容得大意，關鍵字是"What" can I do for you? 和後面接著的答話。

Question 2： What does the woman offer to do for the man?
A. To close the bank account.
B. To lend the man some money.
C. To borrow money from the bank.
D. To stop the transaction of the card.

問題2：這女子主動提出要為這男子做什麼？
A. 將銀行帳戶關掉。
B. 借一些錢給這個男子。
C. 向銀行借一些錢。
D. 為信用卡辦理止付。

答案：D

本題是屬於細節性問題，只要聽到對話最後部分這兩人的一問一

答，便能得到答案。

◎Long conversation　長篇對話

範例：

M1："You two are going to be our sales representatives in the United States. One is to go to the cities on the Eastern Coast, and the other is to go to the cities on the western side. How are you two going to decide on which place to go?"

W："To be fair with each other, I think we should draw lots to decide on it."

M2："That won't be necessary. Angel, since you studied in California before, I think you understand the western cities in the States much better than I do. For the overall performance of our company, we should let you go there. As for me, it is my first time to visit the States, so any city is new to me anyway."

W："That's very nice of you, Kevin."

M2："Have you forgotten? I am the kind of person who likes challenges."

M1： "Good, young man. That matter is now solved. As I told you before, the commission you'll get is 20% of the sale of each sports product."

W： "Is it possible for us to get 25% if our sales exceed 500 items?"

M2： "What about 30% for more than 700 items?"

M1： "Both of you are very confident in your capability as a salesperson, but your business trips last only 10 days. Do you really think you can sell that many items? How about both of you keep close contact with me via Skype and let me know how your business is going every day. If your sales hit 500, then we can start talking about raising the commission."

W： "That sounds good."

M2： "I think so, too. Thank you."

中文翻譯：

第一位男子：「你們兩位要代表本公司到美國當業務代表。一位要到東岸的城市，另一位要到西部城市。你們要如何決定誰去哪裡？」

女：「為了對彼此公平起見，我認為應該抽籤來決定。」

第二位男子：「沒有這個必要。安琪兒，既然妳從前曾經在加州求學，我想妳對美國西部城市比我還了解。為了公司整體的表現，應該讓妳去那裡。對我而言，這是我第一次到美國，無論哪個城市對我都是全新的。」

女：「凱文，你人真好。」

第二位男子：「妳忘了嗎？我是喜歡挑戰的那種人。」

第一位男子：「年輕人，很好，這個問題現在解決了。就像我告訴過你們的，你們每賣出一個運動產品，就可以得到20%的佣金。」

女：「要是我們的銷售量超過500，能得到25%的佣金嗎？」

第二位男子：「要是超過700，能得到30%的佣金嗎？」

第一位男子：「你們兩位都對自己的推銷能力都很有信心，但是你們的商務旅行只有十天，你們真的認為可以賣出這麼多產品嗎？你們兩個何不透過Skype和我保持密切聯絡？好讓我知道你們每天生意進展如何。如果你們的銷售量超過500，我們再來開始討論提高佣金。」

女：「聽來不錯。」

第二位男子：「我也是這麼認為，謝謝。」

Question 1: What is the topic of discussion in the beginning of this conversation?

A. Which place to go for postgraduate studies.

B. Which person to go to which parts of the States.

C. Which date to depart for a business trip.

D. Which city to launch their new products in.

問題1：這段對話剛開始在談論什麼主題？

A. 該去什麼地方念研究所。

B. 如何決定誰去美國的什麼地方。

C. 哪一天出發去出差。

D. 要在哪一個城市發表新產品。

答案：B

這類長篇談話的問題一般都是按照內容順序來問問題的，所以這裡的第一題便問這段對話剛開始的問題。如果先掃讀了本題目，在聆聽的時候便會特別注意相關的關鍵字，馬上知道重點為：”How” are you two going to decide on which place to go? 和後面接著的答話。

Question 2： What are Angel and Kevin negotiating with their supervisor?

A. Discount.

B. Tax.

C. Promotion.

D. Commission.

問題2：安琪兒和凱文和主管協商什麼？

A. 折扣優惠。

B. 稅金。

C. 促銷。

D. 佣金。

答案：D

這對話內容提到了commission（佣金）和數字，而數字一向是關鍵重點，所以不難判斷出答案。

Question 3: On what basis are the two salespeople bargaining with their supervisor?

A. The promotion rallies they will set up.

B. The quantities of items they will sell.

C. The trade fairs they will attend.

D. The numbers of cities they will visit.

問題3：這兩位推銷員是以什麼為標準來和主管協商？

A. 他們將進行的促銷活動。

B. 他們所賣出的數量。

C. 他們會出席的商展。

D. 他們會拜訪的城市數目。

答案：B

這一題承接上一題而來，如果聽懂了關於數字（關鍵字）的討論，也就能答對了。

Question 4: How will the two salespeople keep in contact with their supervisor in Taiwan?

A. By telephone.

B. Via e-mail.

C. Via Skype.

D. By text messages.

問題4：這兩個業務代表將如何和他們在台灣的主管保持聯絡？

A. 電話。

B. 電子郵件。

C. Skype。

D. 簡訊。

答案：C

這是屬於細節性問題，如果夠專心聽，不難於對話快結束前聽到這個答案。

Question 5：For the time being, the commission they agree upon is?

A. 30%

B. 25%

C. 20%

D. 15%

問題5：目前他們所同意的佣金是？

A. 30%

B. 25%

C. 20%

D. 15%

答案：C

這一題難度偏高，必須要能完全聽明白他們三人協商的結果，才能

正確作答。如果先掃讀了此題目，心裡已有準備會出現數字的細節問題，而且本題目內已告知要測驗的就是佣金，那麼便不會有太大問題了。

◎Short talk　簡短談話

範例：

(Announcement) Spokesperson of an airline company:

"All passengers waiting for Star Airline, may I have your attention please: Due to an approaching super typhoon, Typhoon Henry, all of our flights this evening and tomorrow morning will be canceled. Please pay close attention to the latest information on the Arrival and Departure Board and to the announcement as well. If there is any difference between the two new updates, please follow the announcement. Please understand this is done for the safety of all passengers. Thank you for your understanding and cooperation."

中文翻譯：

（廣播）某家航空公司的發言人：

「所有等候搭乘星辰航空的乘客請注意：因為亨利超級颱風的逼

近，我們所有今晚和明天上午的班機將全部取消。請密切注意班機時刻表還有廣播。如果這兩者之間的最新消息有差異，請以廣播為準。請明白這樣的安排是為了所有乘客的安全。感謝您的體諒和合作。」

Question 1: What is the main idea of this announcement?
A. To make passengers aware of the safety of their flights.
B. To make passengers spend more time shopping.
C. To attract more holiday takers to fly their Airline.
D. To inform the passengers of the cancelation of the flights.

問題1：這廣播主要內容是什麼？
A. 請乘客了解班機安全的重要性。
B. 讓乘客多花一點時間購物。
C. 吸引更多的渡假客搭他們航空公司的班機。
D. 告知乘客班機將取消。

答案：D
本題是考主旨的問題，聽到了大意即可得分。

Question 2: According to the spokesperson, what should passengers do if the updates on the board are different from the announcements?

A. Ask the staff at the counter about it.

B. Wait for somebody to explain about the updates

C. Take the announcement as the latest update.

D. Make a wise judgment about the latest update.

問題2：根據這位發言人所說的，如果乘客發現班機時刻表和廣播有差別的話該怎麼做？

A. 向櫃檯人員詢問。

B. 等候他人解説最新消息。

C. 以廣播為最新消息。

D. 明智判斷何者為最新消息。

答案：C

如果聽到了廣播的內容細節便得到這個訊息。

◎Long talk　長篇談話

範例：

With so many Internet providers inundating you with information about their special deals, you could consider yourself lucky to be able to choose from the great packages of our company. In front of you are the PCs connected with our Internet service, which you wouldn't want to miss. Its speed is simply amazing. Not only that, the features of our Internet service include flexible plans, no long-term contracts, and no activation fees. Speaking of the plans, during the demonstration this afternoon, we have the three most popular Internet deals for you:

The first deal is the Ultimate Up to 100 Mbps. This is suitable for home connection with multiple users going online at the same time. Telecommuters and busy households will find this package ideal for them. The price is 897 Taiwan Dollars per month for 12 months.

The second one is the Standard Up to 60 Mbps. It is suitable for web surfing, connecting with friends and family through Facebook, sending e-mails and downloading medium-sized files. 655 Taiwan Dollars per month for 12 months.

The third one is the Basic Up to 24 Mbps. Occasional Internet users will find it suitable for their needs of checking e-mails and sometimes chatting with their friends via Skype.

Aside from that, we also have a special summer deal for families with school children on summer vacation: Those who decide to sign up for one of the three plans mentioned above with me today can get 15 percent off as a special discount.

中文翻譯：

市面上有這麼多提供網際網路的公司不斷對您推銷特別優惠方案，您如果選擇本公司最佳方案就算是您的好運。在您面前展示的是連上我們網際網路服務的桌上型電腦，您一定不想錯過。它的速度非常驚人，除此之外，我們網際網路服務包含彈性時間方案，沒有長時間的綁約，沒有額外的開始費用。說到方案，在今天下午的展示中，我們提供三個最受歡迎的網際網路方案給您：

第一個方案是終極方案，速度高達100 Mbps，這適合家裡多人同時上網。經常上網者和多人同時上網的家庭會覺得這個方案很理想。價格是每個月897台幣，綁約12個月。

第二個方案是標準方案，速度高達60 Mbps，這對於上網很合適，可以用來和朋友、家人玩臉書，傳電子郵件和下載中型的檔案。價格是每個月655台幣，綁約12個月。

第三個方案是基本方案，速度高達24 Mbps，適合偶爾上網者用來查電子郵件、有時和朋友透過Skype聊天。

除此之外，我們有特別適合家中有放暑假的夏天優惠活動：今天決定我和簽訂以上三個方案之一的人，可以得到八五折的優惠。

Question 1： What is the occasion of this long talk?

A. A salesperson is presenting computers for sale.

B. A computer technician is fixing PCs for others.

C. A salesperson is running an Internet demonstration.

D. A programmer is giving a talk to a group of listeners.

問題1：這長篇談話發生的場景是？

A. 一個業務代表正在展示要出售的電腦。

B. 一個電腦技師正在為人修電腦。

C. 一個業務代表正在示範電腦網際網路。

D. 一個程式設計師正在對一群聽眾演講。

答案：C

第一題通常是測驗整體性的問題，例如這裡問場景為何，所以考生最好在聽考題內容前，先快速掃讀問題以獲得大致內容場景和大意。

Question 2: What is NOT one of the features of the Internet service of this company?

A. Many plans for customers to choose from.

B. No contracts over a long time.

C. No starting fees in the beginning.

D. Unlimited telephone calls.

問題2：下列何者不是這家公司網際網路服務的特色之一？

A. 很多可供選擇的方案。

B. 沒有長時間的綁約。

C. 沒有額外的開始費用。

D. 無限制的電話通話。

答案：D

這類細節性問題測驗考生的專注力。

Question 3： Which plan should a mother choose if she has 4 school kids who want to go online at the same time?

A. The Principal.

B. The Basic.

C. The Standard.

D. The Ultimate.

問題3：下列哪個計劃適合家中有四個要同時上網的小孩的媽媽？

A. 主要方案。

B. 基本方案。

C. 標準方案。

D. 終極方案。

答案：D

這裡是測驗考生能不能由一段較長的對話中，快速獲得所需資訊，如果有先掃讀此題目，在聆聽時就能快速聽到正確答案。

Question 4： Which plan should a grandmother choose if she only wants to see photos of her grandchildren on Facebook?

A. The Standard.

B. The Basic.

C. The Ultimate.

D. The Principal.

問題4：只想要看孫子孫女臉書的祖母應該選哪一個方案？

A. 標準方案。

B. 基本方案。

C. 終極方案。

D. 主要方案。

答案：A

技巧如上，務必先掃讀考題。

Question 5: If someone with children in school decides to purchase an Internet plan on that day with the salesperson, what is the discount?

A. 95% of the price.

B. 90% of the price.

C. 85% of the price.

D. 80% of the price.

問題5：如果某個有小孩的人決定當天向業務代表購買網際網路服務，折扣如何？

A. 價格的95%。

B. 價格的90%。

C. 價格的85%。

D. 價格的80%。

答案：C

因為先掃讀了此題，知道於內容結束前會出現數字性問題，便會專注聽數字這個關鍵字。

◎Graph　圖表

請先掃讀測驗題目，尋找與圖表相關的線索。

由圖表的標題來判斷內容。

重點在於迅速掌握圖表，獲得所需資訊，無須細讀。

範例：

The following graph represents the performances of each branch office of a company for four seasons.

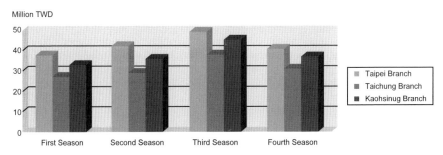

各分公司於四季中的表現

Question 1: Which branch office had the best performance of all three cities listed in all seasons?

A. Taipei branch.

B. Taichung branch.

C. Kaohsiung branch.

D. Not mentioned here.

問題1：哪一家分公司於四季中都有最佳的表現？

A. 台北分公司。

B. 台中分公司。

C. 高雄分公司。

D. 這裡沒提及。

答案：A

這一題說明了只要先讀題目和圖表，聽懂問題，立刻得分。

Question 2： Which branch office had the lowest business volume in all four seasons?

A. Taipei branch.

B. Taichung branch.

C. Kaohsiung branch.

D. Not mentioned here.

問題2：哪一家分公司於四季中的營業額都是最低？

A. 台北分公司。

B. 台中分公司。

C. 高雄分公司。

D. 這裡沒提及。

答案：B

技巧如上一題。

Question 3： In which season did all three branch offices
hit the highest record of business?
A. The first season.
B. The second season.
C. The third season.
D. The fourth season.

問題3：在哪一季中三家分公司的表現都最佳？
A. 第一季。
B. 第二季。
C. 第三季。
D. 第四季。

答案：C

這一題則是要稍微研究一下圖表才能得到答案。因為企業英檢是英
語能力測驗，所以會考的圖表都在一般人能理解的範圍內，所以不
必特別花時間和心力去準備。

◎ News Headlines

For questions 1 to 5, you will hear five news reports. After you hear each news report, choose the headline from the list that best matches the news report you have heard.

新聞標題：第 1 到 5 題為五篇新聞報導；每題請聽光碟放音機播出的新聞報導後，從試題冊上 7 個選項中選出對應的標題。

在「聽新聞，選標題」的這項測驗中，務必要先讀選項，也就是對應的標題，如此才可迅速掌握關鍵字，於聆聽新聞時快速將標題正確配對，同時將多餘標題篩選掉。

範例：

1. According to recent surveys, more and more school children in Taiwan have a mother who is not from Taiwan. These kids often face discrimination one way or another, especially when they do not do as well as the average students or when they do not speak Mandarin as well. Some schools offer after school programs in order to improve their language abilities, but by doing that, these school children with foreign mothers feel they are being segregated from the rest of the class. It is not easy for teachers with large classes to fully address the needs of these students.

2. It is a fact that most movie goers in Taiwan prefer western films to local films. Recently, the success of some local films has triggered a shift in the choices of films to a small degree. Still, several local film makers complain about not being recognized and sponsored for their works. Like almost all other types of art, film-making does not want to compromise quality of the work because of low budgets. Local film makers urge the Ministry of Culture to think more about them when it comes to government funds.

3. The success of organic tea farming in New Zealand is thanks mainly to the contribution of some immigrants from Taiwan. After a series of experimentations, Taiwanese farmers have finally found ways to adapt to the climate of a new country. The British tradition of afternoon tea is very prevalent in the major cities of New Zealand, like Christchurch. More and more Taiwanese tea shops are being set up to provide organic Chinese tea with sweets for afternoon tea. The responses of the general public have been very positive.

4. The gap between the rich and the poor has become wider than before. It is a phenomenon that most economists have noticed for a long time. One obvious reason is that in a

poor family, the budget for education is much lower than in a family with high incomes. Therefore, the poverty is handed down to the next generation. Thanks to public education, some students from poorer backgrounds can have opportunities to succeed in finding good jobs with higher pay - if they are not forced to drop out and take up low-paying jobs before they graduate.

Track 10

5. Due to relatively low average salaries in Taiwan, many Taiwanese young people are opting for working holidays abroad. A recent popular destination is Australia. Reports from the Down Under are both positive and negative. Some regard their working holiday experiences as very rewarding. Most of these positive experiences are as nurses and nannies. Others suffer from occupational damages in jobs such as fruit picking and other labor intensive work. It is generally a good rule to consult with a legal agent about working in Australia to make sure of the conditions of your working holiday visa before departing.

A. More and More Taiwanese Men Seek Partners in China

B. Taiwanese Organic Tea Farming in New Zealand

C. Working Holidays in Australia

D. Internships for Taiwanese Students in Europe

E. The Gap between the Rich and the Poor is Wider than Ever

F. Complaints of Taiwanese Local Film Makers

G. School Children with Non-Taiwanese Mothers

中文翻譯：

1. 根據最新調查結果顯示，台灣有越來越多學齡兒童的母親不是來自台灣。這些小孩經常面臨各式各樣的歧視，特別是那些學科不如一般學生或中文說得不如一般人好的學生。有些學校提供課後輔導來改善他們的語言能力，但是那樣一來，外籍母親的孩子有被與班上其他學生隔離的感覺。班上人數多的老師要完全解決這些學生的問題非常不容易。

2. 台灣大部分看電影的人比較喜歡西洋片，而較不喜歡國片。最近一些國片的成功稍微改變了挑片的口味。但是不少的國片製片者抱怨他們的作品缺乏肯定和贊助。就像其他類型的藝術，電影製片者不願意因為成本低而在作品品質妥協。國片製片者希望文化局在給予政府贊助金時多想想他們。

3. 紐西蘭有機茶業來自於一些台灣移民的貢獻。經過了一連串的實驗後，台灣來的農夫最後總算找到了能夠適應新國家氣候的耕作方式。傳統英國下午茶在紐西蘭主要城市裡非常流行，像是基督城。越來越多的台灣茶商店成立，提供中式有機茶和甜點作為下午茶。大眾的反應非常好。

4.　貧富之間的差距較以前越來越大，這個現象大部分的經濟學者長久以來都已注意到。一個明顯的原因是，在一個貧窮的家庭裡，教育經費相較於所得較高的家庭來得低。因此，貧窮就一代一代傳了下去。因為有公立學校教育，有些家境較差的學生能夠有機會找到薪水較高的職業——如果他們沒有被迫在中途休學，做薪水較低的工作。

5.　因為台灣薪水相對較低，很多台灣年輕人選擇到國外打工度假，其中最近很受歡迎的目的地是澳洲。從澳洲傳來的報導有正面的也有負面的。有些認為他們的打工度假經驗很值得，大部分這些正面的經驗是當護士和保姆。有的人則是在採水果和其他勞力密集的工作受到了職業傷害。大體而言，最好向合法仲介諮詢打工度假事項，以在出發前了解打工度假簽證的條件。

A.　越來越多台灣男人在中國尋找配偶

B.　在紐西蘭的台灣有機茶業

C.　台灣學生在歐洲的實習機會

D.　貧富之間的差距較以前越來越大

E.　台灣國片製片者的抱怨

F.　外籍母親的學齡兒童

答案：1. (G)　　2. (F)　　3. (B)　　4. (E)　　5. (C)

+MP3

Chapter.

03

閱讀講座

Mastering the GEPT Pro
The General English Proficiency Test
Professional

史上最強 GEPT Pro 企業英檢一本就夠

1. 閱讀重點：

◎相較於聽力測驗，時間管理在閱讀測驗更形重要，聽力測驗中只要跟上播音速度即可，但是在閱讀測驗如果沒有將時間分配好就可能無法完成所有題目，憑白失去不少分數。

◎為快速作答，略讀（skimming）與掃讀（scanning）是必備的技巧：
◆略讀（skimming）：快速瀏覽全文，以獲得大意。
◆掃讀（scanning）：快速掃描整篇文章，以獲得特定的細節性資訊。

◎下列題目常出現：
◆一般性題目，問主旨、目的類。
◆特定性題目：◇Who問題，例如：這封電子郵件收件人可能是誰？／這位先生的職位可能是？
◇單字問題，例如：內文中的某個單字是什麼意思？
◇細節的推論問題，例如：由文中可知截稿日期是什麼時候？
◇NOT問題，例如：下列關於這個會議的敘述何者不是正確的？

◎略讀與掃讀的技巧應用：閱讀文章前，務必先快速讀完題目以及四個選項。

◆如果四個選項皆包含人名、數字等明顯的關鍵字，則快速掃讀全文以搜尋正確的人名、數字答案。

◆如果四個選項較長，並非只是人名、數字等明顯的關鍵字，則應以問題中的關鍵字（例如人名或職稱、時間或金錢的數字、地點等等）來掃讀全文，通常在文中關鍵字的上下文稍作推論，即可找到答案。

◎因為這個英文測驗答錯不倒扣分數，所以若不知正確答案，也應隨意選個答案，不要不答。

2. 常見的格式與內容：

◎Form　表格

範例：

Judy Kao

Judykao@gmail.com
12F, No. 108, Zhongshan Rd, Sanchong District,
New Taipei City, Taiwan
(02) 2898 5325

Date of Birth: Feb. 27, 1982

Position sought: Event manager

Experiences: 2010 - 2013 Spokesperson for British Council
2008- 2010 Extracurricular activity Organizer for European School
in Taipei

Education: National Taiwan University, MA in Journalism
One year as an exchange student at Oxford University

Reference: Dr. Richard Ellis, Director of the British Council
Dr. Wen-yi Ma, head of the Journalism Department
(National Taiwan University)

中文翻譯：

茱蒂·高

Judykao@gmail.com
台灣新北市三重區中山路108號12F
(02) 2898 5325

生日：1982年2月27日

申請職位： 活動經理

經歷： 2010 - 2013 英國文化協會發言人
2008- 2010 歐洲學校課外活動負責人

教育背景： 國立台灣大學‧新聞碩士
曾經一年於牛津大學當交換學生

推薦人： 英國文化協會主任：艾理查先生
國立台灣大學新聞系系主任：馬文義博士

1. What is this form for?

A. It is a list of staff members.

B. It is a resume.

C. It is a personal e-mail.

D. It is a To-Do List.

問題1：這張表格是什麼樣的表格？

A. 員工名單。

B. 履歷表。

C. 私人電子郵件。

D. 待辦事項單。

答案：B

這是一般性題目，問這個表格的目的，只要快速略讀此表格，即可判斷出是履歷表。

2. Who might be the receiver of this form?
A. The head teacher of the European school.
B. The director of the British Council.
C. The head of the Journalism Department.
D. The Human Resources manager of an organization.

問題2：誰可能是這張表格的收信者？
A. 歐洲學校的主任教師。
B. 英國文化協會的主任。
C. 新聞系系主任。
D. 某個機構的人力資源經理。

答案：D

這是特定性題目Who問題，如果判斷出這是張履歷表即可答對。

3. What is NOT mentioned in this form?
A. The age of the applicant.
B. The job the woman applies for.
C. The work experiences the woman had

D. The pay the applicant expects.

問題3：下列何者在這張表格內沒有提及？

A. 申請者的年紀。

B. 這位女子要申請的工作。

C. 這位女子的工作經驗。

D. 這位申請者期待的薪水。

答案：D

這是特定性題目NOT問題，只要掃讀表格內標題就可以得知並沒有
薪水這一項目。

◎Minute　會議紀錄

範例：

Minutes of Meeting

Company： Sunshine Beauty Salon

Date： September 17, 2013

Time： 9am to 11am

Venue： Meeting Room, Head Office

Attendee：

Robert Johnson, Branch Manager

Vicky Lee, Head Supervisor

Jeff Wang, Training Consultant

Wangli, Lin, Marketing Executive

Jennifer Chen, Secretary

Agenda:

General discussion

Internship and recruitment

Training programs

1. General discussion: This is a broad discussion to evaluate the performance of the company in the first half of the year 2013. General questions like the direction of the company, corporate mission and image, team spirit and so on are to be discussed here.

2. Internship and recruitment: This discussion is aimed toward developing a new hiring policy and giving young people internship opportunities.

3. Training programs: In this section, the focus of the discussion is to develop sound training programs and career plans for all staff, including interns.

Meeting was adjourned at 11am. Next meeting is scheduled a month from now, i.e. October 17, 2013, same venue and time. Feedback on each discussion topic is to be presented.

Minutes prepared by： Jennifer Chen

中文翻譯：

公司：陽光美髮院

日期：2013年9月17日

時間：上午9點至11點

地點：總公司會議室

出席者：

分公司經理：羅伯特・強森

主管：薇琪・李

訓練諮商師：傑夫・王

行銷主任：林旺利

秘書：珍妮佛・陳

議題：

總討論

實習機會和徵人

培訓計劃

1. 總討論：這是評估公司於2013上半年表現的整體討論。公司方向、企業使命和形象、企業精神等大綱性的問題會於此提出討論。

2. 實習機會和徵人：這討論是以建立新的雇聘政策和提供年輕人實習機會為目標。

3. 培訓計劃：在這個部分，討論的焦點是發展完善的培訓計劃和生涯規劃以提供給全體工作人員，包含實習生。

上午11點休會，下次會議安排於一個月後，也就是2013年10月17日，同一地點同一時間。屆時請提出關於所有討論的意見。

會議由珍妮佛‧陳所紀錄

1. What is the purpose of this writing?
A. To reduce the expenses of a company.
B. To record the contents of a meeting.
C. To draw new talents to join the team.
D. To advocate the mission of the company.

問題1：這文件的目的為何？
A. 減少公司開銷。
B. 紀錄會議內容。
C. 吸引新人材進入公司。
D. 提倡公司使命。

答案：B
這是一般性題目，問這篇文字的目的，只要快速略讀此文，即可判斷出是會議紀錄。

2. What is the topic of the general discussion in this

meeting?

A. Development of hiring strategies.

B. Innovation of a training program.

C. Evaluation of past performance.

D. Solving problems with effective strategies.

問題2：這會議的總討論主題為何？

A. 建立新的雇聘政策。

B. 創立培訓計劃。

C. 評估過去表現。

D. 以有效策略解決問題。

答案：C

這是特定性題目，考的是細節，因為選項皆略長，所以由題目中找

到關鍵字：「總討論」（General discussion），掃讀全文，在

General discussion後面馬上找到了答案：評估過去表現。

3. What time will they gather again to discuss the feedback?

A. It's not mentioned here.

B. In a week.

C. In a month.

D. On Nov. 17.

問題3：下次什麼時後他們會再開會討論意見？

45

A. 這裡沒有提及。

B. 再過一星期。

C. 再過一個月。

D. 11月17日。

答案：C

先快速讀完題目和選項，因為選項都是時間，所以可以馬上掃讀全
文提到時間的地方，而本題也無須多推論就可得到正確答案：再過
一個月。

◎Graph　圖表

範例：

The Number of Bookstores with PCs in Taichung

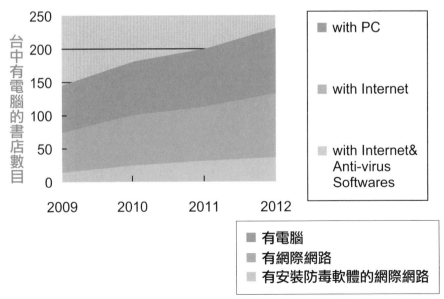

1. What does this graph show us?

A. Many people in Taichung do not have Internet at home.

B. The number of bookstores with Internet is increasing in Taichung.

C. The importance of anti-virus software cannot be overlooked.

D. All bookstores in Taichung have Internet Service.

問題1：這張圖表説明了什麼？

A. 台中很多人在家沒有網際網路。

B. 台中有網際網路的書店在增加中。

C. 防毒軟體的重要性不可忽視。

D. 所有台中的書店都有網際網路服務。

答案：B

圖表只要略讀以求得其用意即可，不需要知道所有細部資訊。這題是一般性題目，問這個圖表的大致內容。標題在圖表中提供了重要資訊：「台中有電腦的書店數目」和旁邊的文字敍述告訴我們這圖表要表達的資訊，加上歷年來曲線皆上揚，可知都是處於增加的趨勢，所以很快知道答案為B。

2. What can be inferred from this graph?

A. All Internet users have anti-virus software in Taichung.

B. Internet service is installed on all PCs in Taichung.

C. Bookstores with Internet service have been the trend in Taichung.

D. All Internet users have PCs at home in Taichung.

問題2：從這張圖表可以推論出什麼？

A. 台中所有的網路使用者都有防毒軟體。

B. 台中所有的電腦都有網際網路服務。

C. 台中的書店流行有網際網路服務。

D. 所有台中的網路使用者在家都有電腦。

答案：C

因為有網際網路的書店數目明顯在增加當中，所以可推論這是一種流行，所以答案為C。

3. What can be said about the data in the year of 2012?

A. More than half of the Internet comes with anti-virus software.

B. Most people prefer going to Internet cafés than bookstores.

C. Many bookstores are closed because people can buy books online.

D. More than half of the bookstores with PCs have Internet service.

問題3：根據2012年的數據，可以推論什麼？

A. 超過半數的網路有安裝防毒軟體。

B. 大多數人較喜歡網咖,而較不喜歡書店。

C. 很多書店結束營業,因為人們在網路購書。

D. 超過半數書店的電腦有提供網路服務。

答案:D

這是特定性題目,同時需要正確推論才可以得到細節答案。在圖上可看出只有極少數網路有安裝防毒軟體,不超過半數,所以選項A不成立,選項B和C與圖表無關,如果用刪去法(刪去錯誤選項),亦可得知選項D為正確答案;為了謹慎起見,還是要讀選項D,在圖上可以清楚看到,超過半數書店的電腦有提供網路服務,所以為正確答案。

◎E-Mail　電子郵件

◆電子郵件是經常測驗的項目，務必注意寄件人和收件人資訊，例如職稱和公司等等。

◆主旨告知信中內容大意，所以非常重要。

◆關於日期和金錢的數字還有地點都很重要。

範例：

From：Rebecca Chang

To：Happy Holiday Travel Agency

Subject：Trip to Tokyo (July 22 to July 26, 2013)

Date：Thursday, August 29, 2013 10：38：27 a.m.

Dear Mr. Chen,

From July 22 to July 26, 2013, I went on one of your package tours for parents and their preschool children to Tokyo, Japan. During the 5 days and 4 nights, our accommodation was in an old run-down hotel with most parts of the inside under renovation. The quality of the breakfast buffet in the hotel was terrible. Not only that, during this organized tour, we were taken mostly to Chinese restaurants, instead of the traditional Japanese cuisines as listed in the itinerary plan. The only one

Japanese eatery we were taken to was shabby and dim, which was far from the fancy restaurant of which we were told.

Your spokesperson told us 3 weeks ago that you would ask the responsible Japanese travel agency to apologize and to pay for our loss, but so far we have not been informed of any new development. Please do regard our complaints seriously and take immediate measures.

Thank you very much.

Best Regards,

_____

Rebecca Chang
Nature Kindergarten
Tel：2784 5621 ex 16
Email：rebeccachang@hotmail.com

_____

中文翻譯：

電子郵件

寄件者：羅貝卡‧張
收件者：快樂假期旅行
主旨：東京之旅（2013年7月22日至7月26日）
日期：2013年8月29日星期四上午10：38：27

陳先生：

2013年7月22日至7月26日我參加了貴旅行社的東京親子遊。在五天四夜的行程中，我們所下榻的飯店破舊不堪，有些飯店內部還在整修。飯店自助早餐的品質非常差。除此之外，我們所到的餐廳幾乎都是中式的，並非行程中所列的日本傳統餐點。唯一一家我們所到的日式餐館非常破舊且昏暗，一點也不像原先我們被告知的豪華餐廳。

你們的發言人三星期前告訴我們，你們會請日本負責的旅行社道歉並賠償損失，但是到目前為止我們沒有得到最新消息。請正視我們的抱怨，馬上採取行動。

謝謝

順頌商祺
————————————
羅貝卡‧張
大自然幼兒園

電話：2784 5621轉16

電子信箱：rebeccachang@hotmail.com

_____

1. Why does the person write this e-mail?

A. To get a discount.

B. To lodge a complaint.

C. To discuss travel plans.

D. To win a free trip.

問題1：這個人為什麼寫這封信？

A. 為了得到折扣。

B. 為了申訴。

C. 為了討論旅遊計劃。

D. 為了贏得免費旅程。

答案：B

這是一般性題目，問這封電子郵件的目的，只要快速瀏覽本信，即可得知是關於客訴問題。

2. The meaning of the word "itinerary" here is close to which of the following?

A. A record of places traveled.

B. An agreement of package tours.

C. A detailed plan for a journey.

D. An activity for parents with kids.

問題2：「行程」這個字在這裡和下列何者意思最接近？

A. 去過地方的紀錄。

B. 套裝行程的合約。

C. 具體的旅遊計劃。

D. 親子活動。

答案：C

測驗單字其實是在測驗分析上下文的能力，而由這裡的上下文得知，意思應該是選項C：具體的旅遊計劃。

3. What is the response of the Taiwanese travel agency so far?

A. They are not going to do anything about it.

B. They have not responded to that matter.

C. They avoid mentioning compensation.

D. They will make the Japanese travel agency pay.

問題3：至今台灣旅行社的反應為何？

A. 他們不會有任何動作。

B. 他們還沒作出反應。

C. 他們避免談及賠償。

D. 他們會請日本旅行社賠償。

答案：D

這是特定性題目，考的是細節的資訊，比起其他題目要花多一點時間，不過只要善用掃讀技巧，即可輕鬆得到答案。

◎Short article（Advertisement） 短文（廣告）

範例：

I would recommend this book titled "The Impacts of Social Media" to anyone who is currently exploring any possibilities with social media. Readers who want to promote a business, an organization or a foundation will find this book particularly useful. The book is like the key to information on social media for beginners and advanced users as well. The case studies in this book are as real as can be for small business owners who look for strategies to navigate the ever increasing social media. Those who wish to study concrete examples of applying social media in business would not be disappointed. As a matter of fact, this book is like the Bible for learning new ways of establishing the image of a company and promoting and marketing a business online.

中文翻譯：

我想要推薦這本書名為《社群網站的影響》的書給任何目前想要探

索社群網站可能性的人。想要宣傳生意、組織、基金會的讀者會特別覺得這本書有用。這本書就像是社群網站新手和老手的資訊鑰匙。本書所提及的個案研究對於在日益增多的社群網站尋找策略運作的小型企業負責人來說，非常貼近現實。想要研究如何在商業中運用社群網站的具體例子的讀者，也絕對不會失望。事實上，這本書就像是學習建立公司形象和網路行銷新方法的聖經。

1. Who are the suitable readers of this book?
A. A chairperson addressing staff in a meeting.
B. Small business owners looking for online marketing strategies.
C. International visitors looking for travel destinations.
D. School children searching for answers in a test.

問題1：這本書對誰適合？
A. 主持員工會議的主席。
B. 尋找網路行銷策略的小型企業負責人。
C. 尋找旅遊目的地的國際旅客。
D. 尋找考試答案的學齡兒童。

答案：B
因為先看了題目和選項，所以很快就發現答案在本文開端，這是屬於Who問題，很多廣告都會點出鎖定的顧客族群。

2. According to this passage, what do the case studies

feature?

A. Latest information.

B. Successful stories.

C. Real examples.

D. Smart solutions.

問題2：根據這篇內容，個案研究有什麼特色？

A. 最新資訊。

B. 成功故事。

C. 真實例子。

D. 聰明解決方法。

答案：C

務必要先看題目和選項，因為case studies明顯是關鍵字，所以快速掃描全文，即可知正確答案為C。

◎Summary Statements　文章段落大意

Task 1: Matching Summary Statements

In each box, five of the six statements are paragraph summaries for the text that follows. Match the statements with the paragraphs. Choose one of the statements from

the list (A-F) for each paragraph. One of the summary
sentences in each box will not be used.

本部份包括兩篇文章，每篇文章分成五個段落。請從方框內的六個
句子中，選出最符合每個段落大意的句子。選項中有一個句子不會
用到。
在這裡務必要先讀選項中的各個段落大意的句子，再略讀文章各段
落，然後才作答。

範例：

A. The director of the Interchange Association (Japan),
Taipei Office, delivered a speech in the beginning of the
fair.
B. It is generally believed that the Japanese Food and
Craft Fair was a successful event.
C. Customers were invited to taste the cuisines and
beverages before their purchases.
D. The Yearly Trade Summit will take place in the Japanese
School in Taipei.
E. The event was a friendly gesture to thank Taiwan for the
help during the 311 Japan earthquake and tsunami in 2011.
F. The fair featured several outstanding masters of food
and craft, who attended the fair.

Japanese Food and Craft Fair in Taipei

1. In order to express gratitude to Taiwanese people for their immediate and generous help during the 311 Japan earthquake and tsunami in 2011, the Interchange Association (Japan), Taipei Office and the Japanese School in Taipei organized a Japanese Food and Craft Fair. The event took place in the Extracurricular Activity Building in the Japanese School in Taipei on July 31, 2013, and was open to the public.

2. The keynote address in the beginning of the fair was delivered by the director of the Interchange Association (Japan), Taipei Office. His short speech summed up the close ties between Taiwan and Japan. Many Taiwanese listeners were reminded of the help from Japan during the 921 Taiwan earthquake in 1999.

3. Many leading masters of food and craft were actually present in the fair along with their works. This special feature of the fair attracted many Taiwanese experts to come to this event as well. It was a common scene to see the Taiwanese and Japanese masters discussing their trade of business.

4. Most of the Taiwanese customers were drawn by the Japanese delicacies. The Taiwanese staff members were students majoring in Japanese and were very enthusiastic in helping customers out. Large quantities of food and beverages were given out for customers to taste before the actual purchases. After enjoying the generous portions for tasting, many customers bought quite a lot to take home.

5. Toward the end of the fair, a group of students from the Japanese School put on a performance of Japanese singing and dancing. Many had Japanese traditional costumes on, and their authentic show really gave the whole event the atmosphere of being in Japan. All in all, the Japanese Food and Craft Fair was regarded by both Japanese and Taiwanese as a great success.

中文翻譯：

文章段落大意

A. 在台日本交流協會主任於展覽前發表了一場演說。
B. 大部分人認為日本美食和技藝展非常成功。
C. 顧客在購買前可以品嚐餐點和飲料。
D. 一年一度的貿易高峰會將在台北日僑學校舉行。

E. 這個活動是為了表達對台灣於日本2011年311強震海嘯賑災的感謝。

F. 好幾位傑出的美食和技藝大師出席了這場盛會，成了活動的特色。

範例：

台北的日本美食和技藝展

1. 為了表達對台灣於2011年日本311強震海嘯慷慨賑災的感謝，在台日本交流協會和台北日僑學校安排了一場日本美食和技藝展。這個展覽於2013年7月31日於台北日僑學校的課外活動中心舉行，所有人都可以參加。

答案：E

2. 於展覽前在台日本交流協主任發表了一場關鍵演說，他的簡短演講對台灣和日本關係作了一個總論，很多的台灣聽眾都想起了日本於1999年921大地震對台灣的協助。

答案：A

3. 很多傑出的美食和技藝大師真的與他們作品一同出席了這場展覽，這個特點吸引了很多台灣專家來到這個盛會。經常可以看到台灣和日本大師一起討論專業知識。

答案：F

4. 大部分台灣顧客是受到日本美食吸引而來的。台灣工作人員為日語系學生，非常樂意幫助顧客。顧客於購買之前，可以先品嚐大量的美食和飲料。在盡情試吃試喝後，很多顧客買了很多食品帶回家。

答案：C

5. 在接近展覽的尾聲時，一群日僑學校的學生表演了日本歌唱和舞蹈，很多穿了日本傳統的衣服，他們道地的表演帶給整個活動日本的氛圍。整體來說，日本美食和技藝展對日本和台灣人來說都是非常成功的盛會。

答案：B

◎Choosing Correct Sentences　文章填空

Task II： Choosing Correct Sentences

Ten sentences have been removed from the two texts that follow. From the sentences in the boxes at the bottom of the pages, choose the sentence that best fits in each gap. One of the missing sentences for each text has been correctly filled in as an example. One of the sentences in each box will not be used.

本部份包括兩篇文章，每篇文章各有四個及六個空格，請由文章下

方方框內提供的選項中，選出正確的句子放回文章空格。每篇文章各標示一句例答供參考。選項中有一個句子不會用到。

這個項目有一定的難度，主要是因為可選句子的主題相似度頗高。要點是務必先讀選項中的各個句子，再略讀文章各段落，在略讀各段落時，找出各段落主旨，然後才將所有選項作最合適的配對。

範例：

How to Learn from a Project?

Many leadership teams often ask themselves, why their planned projects or events ended up in repeated failures. (1)_____. During post-action brain-storming sessions, participants could gain tremendous amounts of problem-solving tactics. In fact, if they learn from the right lessons, they could save lots of time and funds in the next project.

The first question the team leader should ask the team after the event is: What were their expected goals? (2)_____. By constantly reminding them of what they set out to do, all of them would reflect on the whole working process: Did they underestimate the workload involved? Did they take potential risks into consideration? Or were the competitors simply too tough?

The next step is to evaluate the actual result of the project. (3)_____. Disappointment in the team is sometimes inevitable, but a good leader should focus on the morale of the team. Managing expectations is the responsibility of both the team leader and the team players.

The third step is to optimize brainpower in the team in order to pinpoint why there were differences between the desired outcome and the actual outcome. This part is crucial to the positive development of a firm. Sometimes, consultants might be invited in to give suggestions about systemic problems. Instead of finding who is to blame, the team leader should ask the team members to give feedback on their share of work. (4)_____.

If hard-won lessons are not learned, the reviews after any actions would be all in vain. The team leader should serve as a role model for the rest of the team to incorporate what they learned in the past. (5)_____.

中文翻譯：
範例：

如何從專案中學習？

很多領導團隊經常問自己，為什麼所計劃好的專案或活動不斷重覆失敗收場。 (1)_____. 在活動結束後的腦力激盪時段中，參與者能夠得到非常多解決問題的策略。事實上，如果他們學習到正確的教訓，在下次的專案中便得以節省下許多時間和金錢。

領導人應該在活動結束後問團員的是：他們期待的目標為何？ (2)_____. 藉著不斷提醒他們預定要做的是什麼事，他們所有的人便會反省整個工作過程：他們是否低估了會有的工作量？他們是否將潛在風險納入考量？還是競爭對手就是太厲害了？

下一個步驟是要評估這個專案的實際結果。 (3)_____. 對團隊失望在所難免，但是一個好的領導者應該要專注於團隊的士氣。管理期待值是團隊領導人和團員共同的責任。

第三個步驟是要善用團隊的腦力激盪，以確切指出為何理想結果和實際結果會有區別，這個部分對於公司的正面成長非常重要。有時候會請來顧問以獲得系統性問題的建議。領導者不應急著找出該負責的人，而應詢問團員對於所負責工作的意見。 (4)_____.

如果沒有記取辛苦得到的教訓，任何行動後的反省都是徒勞無功的。領導者應該以身作則以作為團員的榜樣，採用他們過去學到的教訓。 (5)_____.

A. Otherwise, the whole process of reviewing would be regarded as a waste of time.

B. Trust and lying cannot coexist in the workplace.

C. With very few exceptions, most outcomes did not turn out as well as expected.

D. After all, each member has contributed to the project and is responsible for the actual outcome.

E. The truth is that they seldom ask their team members to properly review their collaborated actions.

F. In other words, what was the outcome they wanted to achieve?

A. 不然的話，整個反省過程都是浪費時間。

B. 信賴和說謊無法同時在工作場所存在。

C. 除了很少的例外情形，大部分結果不如預期。

D. 畢竟，每個團員都對專案有貢獻，也要對實際結果負責。

E. 事實上，他們很少要求團員好好反省合作的行動。

F. 換句話說，什麼樣的結果是他們原先想要達成的？

答案：1. (C)　　2. (F)　　3. (E)　　4. (D)　　5. (A)

Chapter. 04

第一回
模擬試題

Mastering the GEPT Pro
The General English Proficiency Test
Professional

史上最強
GEPT Pro
企業英檢一本就夠

THE FIRST TEST

LISTENING COMPREHENSION

Part I : Conversations and Short Talks

In Part I, you will hear five conversations and four short talks. Each conversation and talk will be played only once. After each conversation or talk, you will hear one to three comprehension questions. When you hear each question, read the four choices in your test booklet and choose the best answer to the question you have heard.

1.

W : Do you have any work experience in this field?

M : Yes, I had an internship in tourism during last summer vacation.

W : Can you tell me more details?

M : I worked as a tour guide for Japanese tourists.

W : How did it go?

M : I did a great job, and all Japanese visitors loved me.

Question: What industry are these two people talking about?

A. Agriculture.

B. Hospitality.

C. Consulting.

D. Mass media.

2.

M: May I talk to Jack Lin?

W: He is not available at the moment. Would you like to leave a message for Mr. Lin, our manager?

M: Yes, please. I am Tom Wang from United Airline.

W: I'm his secretary. Is there anything urgent I should let him know?

M: Please inform him of the change of his flight tomorrow.

Question: Where does the phone conversation most likely take place?

A. On a business trip.

B. In a travel agency.

C. In a trading company.

D. On an airplane.

3.

M: We have to decide which one to let go.

W: It's a tough decision. What is your opinion?

M: In my opinion, Scott is not doing as well as the others.

W: Do you want my opinion? I don't think any of them deserves to be let go.

M: I understand what you mean, but then you put me in a difficult situation.

Question: What are these two people mainly talking about?

A. Singing contest elimination.

B. Party invitations.

C. Roommate selection.

D. Personnel downsizing.

Track 14

4.

W: May I talk to your manager?

M: Yes, I'm the manager. How can I help you?

W: On Mother's Day I ordered your service to have flowers delivered to my mother. It never happened.

M: That can't be true. Did you order it on the phone?

W: First, I ordered it on your website and then called to confirm it.

Question : What is the main topic of these two people?

A. Suitable gifts for Mother's Day.

B. Customer complaints.

C. High prices of flowers.

D. Special delivery discounts.

5.

Track 15

M : How is your Japan project going so far?

W : So far so good, but I think I'll need more time to do it well.

M : You seem to have finished most of the project. What are your main concerns?

W : It's not among the tasks we talked about, but I'd really like to interview some specialists.

M : As long as you're willing to do extra work, I can give you two more weeks.

Question : What are these two people most likely discussing?

A. Visa renewal.

B. Vacation destination.

C. Work progress.

D. Work permit.

6.

Track 16

W: We are the only company with the know-how to design this translating software for Chinese.

Software like this cannot be found anywhere else online. Our product is the latest development in the field of artificial intelligence for translation. The competitive edge of this product is assured by our programming engineers.

Question 6: What is the main topic in this talk?

A. Latest anti-virus software.

B. Dominating software product.

C. Computer programmer.

D. New computer games.

Question 7: What does "the know-how" mean here?

A. The creativity.

B. The interest.

C. The budget.

D. The knowledge.

Track 17

7.

M: On behalf of our CEO, I'm here to announce that your company was merged with "Serenity" several days ago.

Those of you who wish to work for "Serenity" are invited to schedule a personal meeting with our Manager of the

Human Resource Department by Aug 31, 2013. After that date, it would be assumed that no more original employees are interested in the job vacancies offered by "Serenity".

Question 8: What is the purpose of this short talk?

A. To report a new transition of the company.

B. To show a new CEO around in a branch office.

C. To introduce the new manager.

D. To cut down the costs of Human Resource.

Question 9: What just happened to the company?

A. The company hired new staff.

B. The company launched new products.

C. The company was merged with "Serenity".

D. The company opened a new branch office.

8.

W: The International Exhibition of Laptops is going to take place in Boston, and I'm looking for one more staff member to travel along with me and my interpreter. Whoever considers himself or herself qualified can apply with me. Basic English will be alright because, as I just said, a language specialist will be with us at all times. As you might have heard, a business trip like this could be exhausting. Whoever goes on this business trip can, in return, have a couple days off as soon as we return to Taiwan.

Question 10： What is the main message of this short talk?
A. The annual sales in recent years.
B. The chance of an overseas business trip.
C. The city to visit next month.
D. The client to meet next month.

Question 11： What can be said about the staff members?
A. Most staff members have been on the business trip to Boston.
B. Most staff members like this business trip because they can practice English.
C. Most staff members might know this business trip could be very tiring.
D. Most staff members fight for the opportunities to travel abroad.

Question 12： What can be most likely concluded from this short talk?
A. Nobody will be going on this business trip.
B. Whoever goes on this business trip can get extra days off.

C. This kind of business trip will not happen again in the company.

D. There will be extra money provided for whoever wants to go.

9.

W: James, I really like your presentation. It is very to the point and easy to follow. As I know, this is your first English presentation, and I think overall you did a great job. Maybe you could consider using some graphs next time because visual images can appeal to a wider audience. For a presentation like this, you might want to use pie charts with numbers indicating the sales in each continent.

Question 13: What are these people talking about?

A. The man's English comprehension.

B. The woman's business presentation.

C. The man's first English presentation.

D. The woman's good charts and numbers.

Question 14: What does the woman like about the man's presentation?

A. It is clear and straightforward.

B. It comes with charts and numbers.

C. Its information cannot be found elsewhere.

D. It is creative and hard to copy.

Question 15: What does the woman suggest the man do in his next presentation?

A. To shorten the length of the presentation.

B. To use more quotes from famous people.

C. To use more body language.

D. To use more graphs with numbers.

 Part II: Talks

There are ten questions in this part. Before listening to the recording, you will have 30 seconds to study the graph and read the headlines printed in the test booklet. Each recording will be played just one time.

For questions 16 to 20, you will hear five questions about the male employees' yearly pay vs. female employees' yearly pay in a company on a graph. After you hear each question, choose the best answer to the question you have

heard.

10,000 TWD

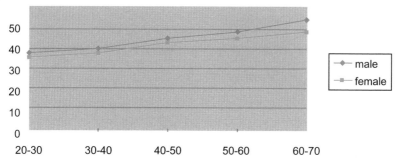

Age of the employees

16. What does this graph represent?

A. The employees' high pay and long years of service in a company.

B. The managerial roles and the employees' ages in a company.

C. The relationships between ages and different tasks they are given.

D. The yearly salaries of male and female staff of different ages in a firm.

17. At what age does an employee probably stop working in this company?

A. 70.

B. 65.

C. 60.

D. 55.

18. What is the relationship between one's salary and one's age in this company?

A. There is no relationship between age and pay.

B. The older one gets, the more pay he or she is likely to get.

C. The older one becomes, the easier his or her work will be.

D. The higher one's salary, the harder it is to get a raise the following year.

19. What can be said about the male employees' yearly pay and female employees' yearly pay?

A. Most female workers are not satisfied with their salaries.

B. Male employees are more efficient and therefore get more pay.

C. Male and female employees must have different work in the company.

D. Male employees earn more than their female colleagues in general.

20. Which best describes the change in an employee's yearly pay in relation to his or her age?

A. Stable and continual growth.

B. Slow and gradual decline.

C. No increase at all.

D. It hits the lowest in the end.

For questions 21 to 25, you will hear five news reports. After you hear each news report, choose the headline from the list that best matches the news report you have heard.

21. Each year, hundreds and thousands of students are interested in studying abroad, but not all of them have sufficient funds to cover tuition fees and the costs of living overseas. Nowadays, more and more banks would like to enter this market of student loans for overseas studies. These banks are considering extending the age limit and providing more people, who are interested in studying abroad, access to student loans. The Ministry of Education is carefully evaluating the proposals of these banks.

22. More than 400,000 people have used U-Bike so far in Taipei, including locals and international visitors. Most of them are very satisfied with the first 30-minute free ride; some complain about not having a spot when they

return the U-Bike. There are also people who ride the U-Bike a bit too far and therefore have to face penalties. Overall, almost all U-Bike users are positive that they will use U-Bike as frequently as situations allow.

Track
23

23. Wooden buildings have become the increasingly popular choice of modern architects. The costs of building such green architecture often involve the accompanying solar panels and water recycling devices. In the long run, it actually costs less to maintain such a building. The Beitou City Municipal Library is one of the successful examples of such a green building made of wood. It has won international acclaim and has attracted many visitors. Living in harmony with nature is what most architects of green wooden buildings believe in.

Track
24

24. Products made of recycled resources are not rare, but have you seen products made of recycled bicycle parts? Like all other items in the world, a bicycle has its limited time of service. There inevitably comes a day when the owner has to see the beloved bicycle enter the dump ground. For this, a Dutch bicycle shop owner came up with the idea of making old bicycle parts into everyday products, such as tables, chairs and shelves. Soon the idea spread into other parts of the world, and now many

bicycle experts are catching on to this trend.

25. Many teenagers commit crimes due to their pasts of being abused. This January, the authorities concerned set up several new workshops to help these young people. Some of the youngsters who committed juvenile delinquency are not violent in nature, and they are advised to make some handcrafted works and other products like soap. In such a protected working environment, they can regain self-esteem, and the money generated from their handmade products can help them pay for their basic living costs. It is a win-win situation for these young men and young women, who often just got out of youth detention centers.

A. Buildings Made of Wood are Environmentally Friendly

B. More and More Banks Want to Give out Student Loans

C. Authorities Concerned are Rethinking about Urban Renewal

D. Recycled Products Made of Old Bicycle Parts

E. U-bikes are Popular among Locals and Visitors alike

F. Opportunities for Foreign Architects in Taiwan

G. Workshops for Abused Teenagers

Part III: Long Talk & Long Conversation

In Part III, you will hear one long talk and one long conversation. Each of them will be played only once. Before you listen to each talk or conversation, you will have 45 seconds to read the questions printed in the test booklet. After hearing the recording, you will have one minute to answer the questions. Choose the correct answer from the choices A, B, C, or D.

(1)

M: Next week we'll be taking part in the International Lighting Product & Technology Exhibition in Seattle. As previous experiences in such an international fair showed, most foreign companies are particularly interested in our two special areas: First, the uniquely designed LED Light Tiles, featuring built-in optics, ultra thinness, low weight and high efficiency. The other attractive area, which always draws huge crowds of visitors for our company, is the office lighting products. Most of you have participated and contributed in the process of designing, researching and developing our award-winning LED lighting designed products. Now it is your opportunity to proudly

present your marvelous works to international experts and consumers. Study all of our products in the catalogs carefully for this exhibition because chances are you will frequently be asked about the lighting products, which are not designed by you. All of you are expected to be able to answer any question at any time. You should support each other as a team even more so abroad than in Taiwan. While I have no doubt in your English communication ability in this industry, I suggest you to hone your language skills by listening to English radio news every day from now on. I have confidence in all of you, and I am sure you will learn a lot from this experience and benefit immensely from the business partners you'll make in this event in the States.

26. What is the main topic of the speaker?

A. Researching grants and scholarship.

B. An international Lighting Exhibition.

C. Design and life styles.

D. Industrial revolution.

27. Who are the listeners most likely to be?

A. CEOs of different lighting companies.

B. Designers of LED lighting products.

C. Manufacturers of LED lighting plants.

D. Salespeople of LED lighting devices.

28. What does the speaker expect his listeners to do before going to the exhibition?

A. Make contacts.

B. Read newsletters.

C. Study catalogs.

D. Book flights.

29. In this talk, the word "hone" is closest in meaning to which of the following?

A. Listen.

B. Polish.

C. Grow.

D. Understand.

30. What is the general tone of the speaker in this talk?

A. Reluctant.

B. Condescending.

C. Encouraging.

D. Sympathizing.

(2)

Manager： Jason, this is Ann from the U. K. Ann, this is Jason and he is an expert in economic issues in Taiwan. Ann just finished her market researching in Taitung. I'd like you two to share with us your opinions on the marketing strategies of new products in the eastern part of Taiwan.

Jason：Nice to meet you, Ann. Why don't you start first by telling us your observations of markets in Taitung?

Ann：During my 7-day stay in Taitung, I visited the potential retailers of our various products of chocolates and other sweets. Aside from that, I had meetings with the owners of major supermarkets and listened to their advice and feedback.

Jason：What does the future of our sweets from England look like in Taitung?

Ann：The prospects of our chocolates and other sweets are very promising. Although the customers complain about the rising prices of western food, like Subway, most of them remain loyal customers. Since a western brand, like

Subway, with such an increase in price can make profits in Taitung, our refined products surely can enter the market now. The truth is that most people there are confident in the quality and reputation of most western delicacies.

Jason：In the case of Subway, its marketing scheme has taken quite some time to be effective. Other western fast food chains have also spent a huge amount of money on advertisement in the media. What makes you so sure that we as an English brand can win consumers in this new market in eastern Taiwan?

Ann：I'm sure that you will all agree with me that our English brand has an excellent reputation in the world. Nobody can deny its leading share of our domestic market in the U.K. We should never underestimate the buying power of the residents there.

Jason：What you just said is close to my observation of the market from the media. Thank you very much for sharing your insights with us.

Manager：In that case, I think we can all anticipate the appearance of our products on the eastern market very soon.

31. What subject does the manager want Jason and Ann to discuss?

A. Buying supermarkets in Taitung.

B. Visiting a chocolate factory in Taitung.

C. Marketing their products in Taitung.

D. Opening a branch office in Taitung.

32. What does Ann think the outlook of their products looks like?

A. Hopeful.

B. Downward.

C. Weak.

D. Tragic.

33. Why does Ann compare Subway in Taitung to their products?

A. They both have many customers.

B. They both just raised the prices.

C. They both were once popular.

D. They both are western brands.

34. Why does Jason agree with Ann on her opinions?

A. It is reflected in the recent sales.

B. It matches with his observation.

C. It corresponds to the marketing plans.

D. It shows in the English domestic market.

35. What is the conclusion in this discussion?

A. They will invest lots of money for chain stores.

B. Their chocolates will be marketed in the U.S.A.

C. They will do more marketing researches in Taitung.

D. Their products will be launched soon in eastern Taiwan.

READING COMPREHENSION

Part One : Charts, Letters and Short Essays

In this part of the test, you will find charts and several passages. Each chart or passage is followed by two to four questions. You are to choose the BEST answer, A, B, C or D, to each question on the basis of the information provided in the chart or passage. Then, on your answer sheet, find the number of the question and mark your answer.

(1)

Customer Satisfaction Survey

To ensure we provide the best service we can, we would appreciate if you can help us with the following questionnaire.
The details of your information will only be used by Getaway Travel Agency staff.

General Information

NAME:	Wendy Chang
COMPANY:	QSquare Shopping Center
PHONE: (02)2367-3325	MOBILE: 0942-553-256
E-MAIL:	Wendyc0110@hotmail.com
Date of your most recent contact with us?	June 15, 2013

How would you rate your overall satisfaction with us?

__ Highly dissatisfied
✓ Somewhat dissatisfied
__ Neutral
__ Somewhat satisfied

___ Highly satisfied

Please rate the following service qualities of our business.

	Very poor	Poor	Neutral	Good	Excellent
Knowledge of staff	___	✓	___	___	___
Helpfulness of staff	___	✓	___	___	___
Range of travel options	___	___	✓	___	___
Tour arrangements	___	___	✓	___	___
Service of tour guide	___	✓	___	___	___

Comment：

> Taiwanese Tour guide's English is too poor. There were too many cases of misunderstanding due to his English skills in communication. The tour arrangements thus left much to be desired.
> The chosen restaurants and hotels were all right.

How likely are you to book with us again?
___ Very unlikely
✓ Somewhat unlikely
___ Neutral

__ Somewhat likely

__ Very likely

How likely will you recommend us to your friends or acquaintances?

✓ Very unlikely

__ Somewhat unlikely

__ Neutral

__ Somewhat likely

__ Very likely

Your feedback is very important to us. Thank you for your time

Questions:

1. What is the main purpose of this questionnaire?

A. To find out where their customers are from.

B. To obtain customer feedback.

C. To find out the incomes of their customers.

D. To hire new employees.

2. What does this customer dislike about the Taiwanese tour guide's service?

A. He does not have sufficient knowledge.

B. He is not helpful enough.

C. He didn't arrange the tour well enough.

D. He couldn't communicate in English well enough.

3. Which of the following is NOT this customer's opinion?

A. The customer is not satisfied with the tour guide.

B. The customer will not come back to the travel agency.

C. The customer complains about the restaurants and hotels.

D. The tour guide in the travel agency need to improve his English.

(2)

June 15, 2013

Internship Opportunities

We are now looking for an intern for the position of school librarian, starting from September 1st, 2013. There is the prospect of becoming a regular employee in the school library in the end of three months of internship. Special training and workshops on the weekend will be provided and as an intern, you will receive the hourly pay

of 115 Taiwan Dollars.

Applicants should possess a degree of Library Science and/or Management of Information Technology. Educational experiences are an advantage for the job vacancy, but not required. Patience, helpfulness and a hard-working spirit in the setting of a school are the ideal qualities of a suitable applicant.

The general job duties are:

-Collaborating with classroom teachers
-Assisting students to search for information in the library
-Encouraging the use of learning technology
-Collecting and analyzing data to improve instruction

Please submit your application by the end of July 31, 2013 and we will announce the result by August 31, 2013 on the official school website.

Jessica Lin
Human Resources Executive

Ba De High School

Tel : (02)2751 2181 Ext. 139

Email : jessicalin@sunshine.com

Questions:

4. What is the main purpose of this notice?

A. To compile a database.

B. To look for interns.

C. To obtain excellent books.

D. To advertise workshops.

5. When is the ending date of the internship?

A. The 1st of September.

B. End of August.

C. End of September.

D. End of November.

6. Which of the following is NOT necessary in applying for the internship?

A. Educational background.

B. Library Science.

C. Database skills.

D. High school certificate.

7. The job description can be best summarized as

A. Training to become classroom teaching staff.

B. Helping school library users.

C. Building a student database.

D. Working in the human resource department.

(3)

From：Alice Wang

To： Tom Brown

Subject： License of "Taipei Stories"

Date： Tue, June 18, 2013 9：18：11 a.m.

Dear Mr. Brown,

Thank you very much for your interest in the license of our book, "Taipei Stories", by Ms. Mary Chang. A copy of the book will arrive at your copyright agency within the next few days.

Since we have never worked with each other before, please give us at least two references of the companies with which your agency has worked in the past. Attached to this

letter is our suggestion of a license agreement. Please
inform us on the specific conditions of the marketing of
the book in your country, so we can fix the license fee
accordingly. In case you would like to change or amend
anything please let me know.

We would be happy to offer some more attractive books for
readers in the U.K. You are welcome to have a look at our
website www.sunshine.com.tw to find out more about our
publishing house. Please go to "Catalogue" on the very
left side of the screen to find information about what we
offer.

In case there are any further questions please do not
hesitate to contact me.

Best Regards,

_____

Alice Wang
Foreign Rights Executive
Sunshine Publishing House
Tel : 2989-6899 Ext. 219

Email: alicewang@sunshine.com

_____

Questions:

8. Why did Ms. Wang write the letter?

A. To buy the license of the book.

B. To have the agency sell the license of the book.

C. To ask for more books from the agency.

D. To complain to the copyright agency.

9. How many references does the publisher require the copyright agency to provide?

A. None.

B. Only one.

C. More than two.

D. No more than two.

10. What is most likely to be found in the attachment?

A. Advertisement.

B. Catalogue.

C. Brochure.

D. Contract.

11. What is NOT true about the e-mail?

A. The copyright agency is interested in books about Taiwan.

B. Ms. Wang wants to sell Taiwanese books to English readers.

C. The publisher and agency have worked before.

D. They are going to talk about the conditions of the copyright.

(4)

July 10, 2013

Notice to All Employees

In order to ensure that our office will be 100% smoking-free zones, we will impose a new regulation regarding smoking beginning July 31, 2013. Those who would like to smoke will no longer be able to do so in the coffee room. Instead they are required to go to the balcony outside of our small kitchen to do so. Whoever smokes in the office or any other areas inside of the building will face penalties. For a first offense in August, 2013, the offender will be given a warning. Second-time offenders will be fined 500 Taiwan Dollars. After September first,

no warnings will be given, and the penalty will be 1000 Taiwan Dollars each time.

We wish all of you great health and a long life.

Alexander Schwarz

General Manager of Asia

Mercedes-Benz Taiwan

Tel： 886-2-27512556 Ext. 19

Email： alexschwarz@bmw.com

Questions:

12. Why did the general manager write the notice?

A. To attract more staff.

B. To announce the new rule.

C. To ask smoking employees to quit their jobs.

D. To make staff quit smoking in a month.

13. Where can one go to if one wants to smoke?

A. The coffee room.

B. The toilet.

C. The balcony.

D. The kitchen.

14. How much will a smoker be fined if caught smoking for the 1st time in the office in September?
A. Zero.
B. 500 NTD.
C. 1000 Taiwan Dollars.
D. Only a warning.

(5)

Timetable of Tai Chi Event

Time	Activities
09:30 to 10:00	Registration & paying membership fees
10:00 to 10:20	Time for catching up
10:20 to 10:40	Presenting awards
10:40 to 11:00	Speeches
11:00 to 12:00	Tai Chi Sports demonstrations
12:00 to 13:30	Lunch over karaoke
13:30 to 13:50	Time to get gifts & ending of the event

Qustions:

15. What is this timetable for?

A. To organize schedules for the boss.

B. To announce the program of the event.

C. To sell sports products.

D. To arrange a fund-raising party.

16. Who are most likely the receivers of the timetable?

A. The singing competitors.

B. The English examinees.

C. The suppliers of sports products.

D. The Tai Chi sports members.

17. What are the possible topics of the speeches?

A. Hiring a personal trainer.

B. Working out in a gym.

C. Tai Chi and health.

D. Singing and its benefits.

Part Two： Essays

Task I : Matching Summary Statements

In each box, five of the six statements are paragraph summaries for the text that follows. Match the statements with the paragraphs. Choose one of the statements from the list (A-F) for each paragraph. One of the summary sentences in each box will not be used.

(1)

A. Some progress has been made regarding some issues of people who are disabled.

B. Most people who are physically and mentally disabled do not want to look for employment.

C. More improvements of employment for people who are disabled can hopefully be made.

D. Many people who are disabled face financial difficulties and the lack of supporting facilities.

E. Most employers are not willing to give applicants who are disabled a chance to work.

F. Job-seekers who are disabled encounter huge obstacles in finding a suitable job.

Employment for People with Disabilities in Taiwan

18. Despite of quite a few government campaigns, the situation of employment for people with disabilities has left much to be desired. Job-seekers who are physically and mentally disabled face unimaginable prejudices and tremendous difficulties in finding suitable jobs, especially in the present economic instability.

19. It is required by law that private-sector employers with 67 or more employees have 1% of the total staff be physically or mentally disabled. If the number of all staff is 67, by law at least one employee must be disabled. Government agencies with 34 or more workers should hire 3% of employees with mental or physical disabilities. Most employers are, however, reluctant to hire applicants who are mentally or physically disabled. Instead, they would rather pay money to a fund set up for employers who are willing to hire more job-seekers with disabilities than required by law. In many cases, those who do hire workers with disabilities often do not pay them adequately for their work.

20. The average incomes of workers who are disabled are

much lower than the national average, and most of them are far below the minimum wage. It means that most of people with disabilities have to depend on their families financially to make ends meet. Many job-seekers who are disabled very often cannot get suitable jobs and have to take whatever work available to earn a living. Most workplaces do not have basic facilities for employees with disabilities, such as those with wheelchairs.

21. Compared to the past, there has been progress made in the areas of health coverage and education for people who are physically and mentally challenged. Currently, almost all people with disabilities are covered in the national health care system, and more and more students who are disabled can go to colleges with special government programs. There have been some, although few, employees with physical and mental disabilities, who manage to earn more than average workers.

22. With more and more widespread schools, particularly colleges, students with disabilities can have more access to learning facilities that cater to their special needs than before. With a gradual change of the general public's perceptions of people with physical and mental disabilities, it is hoped that their work prospects can

be slowly and steadily improved. (Adapted from Taiwan Panorama Magazine, October, 2011)

(2)

A. Indigenous designers' end products are their ways of communicating across cultures.

B. Recently, indigenous Cultural and Creative products have been very successful on the market.

C. It is not easy to tell if an indigenous cultural product is authentic.

D. Employment opportunities have been created because of Indigenous Cultural and Creative products.

E. Indigenous Cultural and Creative products are very unique and thus in high demand.

F. Indigenous products promote self-respect of indigenous people and public perceptions of indigenous culture.

Indigenous Cultural and Creative Products

23. Lately, designed products with indigenous features and images have become very trendy for mainstream customers.

Many of them are considered products of the Cultural and Creative Industry, ranging from table lights with tribal totems to hand-woven bags. All these have been collaborated efforts of indigenous designers, corporate organizations and government decision-makers.

24. Generally speaking, Taiwanese culture is rarely seen internationally, and the indigenous Taiwanese cultures even less so. With the modern products designed with aboriginal features, the awareness of contemporary indigenous culture has been, to a certain extent, elevated. Self-esteem of the indigenous people has therefore been promoted. These cultural aspects of combining art and products have improved the general public's image of the indigenous culture.

25. Job prospects for indigenous job-seekers have typically been on average much dimmer than for others. Many young indigenous people have come to large cities in the hope of finding an ideal job. Only very few of them are lucky enough to be able to get jobs with decent pay and survive in the city jungle. Now with the workshops of indigenous cultural products, many young indigenous people can find internships there and learn useful skills, such as hand-crafting wooden carvings or making designed

desks and chairs. Doing work related to their own tribal heritages has contributed immensely to their own sense of achievement.

26. The uniqueness of indigenous cultural products gives them a competitive edge in the current market. Such rejuvenation of ancient tribal culture has brought fresh vitality to industrial design and attracted all sorts of customers, indigenous and non-indigenous. From international art collectors to souvenir-buying tourists, indigenous designed works have gained interests in Taiwan and abroad.

27. Such products can be a good example of successful the Cultural and Creative Industry. Indigenous designers have brought the revival of their culture, at least in successfully transforming their cultural symbols and images into modern products, which attracts customers' interests. They have initiated cross-communication through their works, and let their tangible items speak for their intangible indigenous culture.

Task II: Choosing Correct Sentences

Ten sentences have been removed from the two texts that follow. From the sentences in the boxes at the bottom of the pages, choose the sentence that best fits in each gap. One of the missing sentences for each text has been correctly filled in as an example. One of the sentences in each box will not be used.

(1)

Adapting novels into movies

As many frequent movie goers might have noticed, the practice of adapting novels into movies has long been a trend in the movie industry.

One of these successful blockbusters is "The Best Exotic Marigold Hotel", which is a 2012 British comedy-drama film. The screenplay was based on the 2004 novel "These Foolish Things". Another example is "Life of Pi", based on the novel of the same title. (28)_____.

Literature experts tend to be concerned about the

quality of the screenplays. (29)_____. To ensure the movie keeps the flavor of the original novel, excellent screenwriting techniques are required. Several seminars and workshops on novel adaptation are offered for whoever wishes to become outstanding screen-writers.

Most English teachers would advise their students read the original novels first and then go to the movie theater afterwards. (30)_____. After all, few can afford the precious time to both read the book and watch the film, not to mention comparing the two to see the differences.

The publishing industry is pleased to find the general public's appetite for reading seems to have revived. (31)_____. Investors see the potential growing market and are willing to promote young beginning screenwriters. To sum up, it is a win-win situation for both the book market and the movie industry.

ANSWERS to choose from :

A. After watching the film adapted from the novel, many people decide to purchase the bestseller to read.
B. Most movie-goers are not keen on films based on famous novels.

C. This movie turned out to be a huge success and has promoted the image of Taiwan.

D. Many people, however, choose to go to the movie, instead of reading the original novel.

E. In other words, they question if the movie retains the essence of the original novel.

(2)

Medical Tourism in Taiwan

Package tours with medical treatments have become recently quite popular. (32)_____. These overseas tourists come to Taiwan for almost all types of medical services, including health check-ups, dental care, cosmetic surgeries and so on. At the same time, they can also enjoy the beautiful scenery of Taiwan.

(33)_____. Taiwan boasts its highly-qualified medical staff and most of whom can speak fluent English, and some Japanese as well. So far, medical tourism in Taiwan has attracted mostly Chinese-speaking patients, such as people from Mainland China and those who live

overseas. Increasingly, countries like the United States and Australia are sending specialists to come to Taiwan to check out the qualities of the medical services offered in Taiwan.

Another reason is the reasonable medical expenses in Taiwan. (34)_____. The medical facilities offer cutting-edge technology which guarantees patients' surgeries and examinations are both time and cost-efficient. With the time and money saved, the medical patients can enjoy themselves by sightseeing or shopping and thus make the most out of their overseas tours in Taiwan.

Taiwan is an ideal place not only for sightseeing, but also for recuperation. Patients who have just gone through an operation need proper rest, and the therapeutic hot springs in resorts are spread almost all around Taiwan. Those who suffer from chronic illness will find natural rehabilitation in the greenery in Taiwan. All around the year, overseas visitors will discover new and old healing appeal on the beautiful island.

Booming medical tourism has brought new opportunities and challenges as well. Quite a few hospitals have already started to work together with airline companies, hotels and resorts to come up with feasible plans to accommodate increasing demands of medical tourists. (35)_____. With 30,000 estimated employee opportunities, the prospects of medical tourism in Taiwan remain quite positive to most residents.

ANSWERS to choose from :

A. Doctors in Taiwan are famous for treating yearlong health problems.

B. Taiwan is undoubtedly one of the leading destinations for medical tourism.

C. One apparent reason is that Taiwan has world-class doctors, hospitals and medical communities.

D. The Immigration Agency has yet to cope with the sudden large influxes of medical tourists.

E. Visitors can have access to such outstanding medical service in Taiwan with substantial financial savings.

Chapter. 04

第一回模擬試題 中文翻譯與解答

Mastering the GEPT Pro
The General English Proficiency Test
Professional

聽力測驗答案

1.	B	11.	C	21.	B	31.	C
2.	C	12.	B	22.	E	32.	A
3.	D	13.	C	23.	A	33.	D
4.	B	14.	A	24.	D	34.	B
5.	C	15.	D	25.	G	35.	D
6.	B	16.	D	26.	B		
7.	D	17.	A	27.	B		
8.	A	18.	B	28.	C		
9.	C	19.	D	29.	B		
10.	B	20.	A	30.	C		

閱讀測驗答案

1.	B	11.	C	21.	A	31.	A
2.	D	12.	B	22.	C	32.	B
3.	C	13.	C	23.	B	33.	C
4.	B	14.	C	24.	F	34.	E
5.	D	15.	B	25.	D	35.	D
6.	A	16.	D	26.	E		
7.	B	17.	C	27.	A		
8.	B	18.	F	28.	C		
9.	C	19.	E	29.	E		
10.	D	20.	D	30.	D		

第一回測驗

聽力測驗
第一部份：簡短對話與談話

本部分包括五篇簡短對話與四篇簡短談話，每篇對話與談話只播出一遍。每篇對話與談話後有一至三個相關的題目。請聽光碟放音機播出問題後，從試題冊上四個選項中選出最適合的答案。

1.

女：你有任何這方面的工作經驗嗎？

男：有，我去年夏天作過旅遊業的實習生。

女：你能告訴我更多的細節嗎？

男：我曾經當過日本觀光客的導遊。

女：結果好嗎？

男：我很稱職，所有的日本觀光客都很喜歡我。

問題：這兩個人在討論哪一行？

A. 農業。

B. 旅遊業。

C. 諮商。

D. 大眾傳播。

答案：B

2.

男：請幫我接傑克・林。

女：他現在沒空，您有什麼要我幫忙轉達給我們林經理嗎？

男：請告訴他我是聯合航空公司的湯姆・王。

女：我是他的秘書。請問您需要留言嗎？

男：請告訴他明天的班機改了。

問題：這通電話最可能在哪裡發生？

A. 商務旅行。

B. 旅行社。

C. 貿易公司。

D. 飛機上。

答案：C

3.

男：我們得要決定要請誰離職。

女：這真是很難的決定，你意下如何？

男：依我看來，史考特表現不如他人。

女：你要聽我的意見嗎？我根本不認為我們該裁員。

男：這一點我明白，但是妳這樣給了我一個大難題。

問題：這兩個人在討論什麼？

A. 歌唱淘汰賽。

B. 舞會邀請名單。

C. 選擇室友。

D. 人事縮編。

答案：D

4.

女：我可以和你們經理談談嗎？

男：可以，我就是經理。有什麼需要我幫忙的嗎？

女：母親節那天我訂了你們的花，還有外送服務，結果沒有收到。

男：不可能，您是否是用電話訂的？

女：首先，我在你們網路訂花，然後再打電話確定。

問題：這兩個人在討論的主題是什麼？

A. 母親節適合的禮物。

B. 顧客抱怨。

C. 花價之高。

D. 特別的外送折扣。

答案：B

5.

男：妳的日本專案進展如何？

女：到目前為止都還不錯，但是我想我需要多一點的時間來把它做得盡善盡美。

男：看來妳已完成了這個專案的大部分。妳還在擔心什麼？

女：這個不在我們討論過的任務範圍內，但是我真的很想要訪問一些專家。

男：要是妳願意做額外的工作，我可以再給妳兩週時間。

問題：這兩個人最可能在討論什麼？

A. 簽證延簽。

B. 旅行目的地。

C. 工作進度。

D. 工作許可。

答案：C

6.

女：我們是唯一一家擁有設計這個中文翻譯軟體技術的公司。像這樣的軟體於線上其他地方沒有辦法找到。我們的產品是這個翻譯之人工智慧領域最先進的發展。我們的程式設計工程師確保這個產品的競爭優勢。

問題6：這談話的主題是什麼？

A. 最新的防毒軟體。

B. 壟斷市場的軟體產品。

C. 電腦程式設計師。

D. 新的電腦遊戲。

答案：B

問題7：在這裡，「技術」的意思是？

A. 創意。

B. 興趣。

C. 預算。

D. 知識。

答案：D

7.

男：我在此代表我們執行長來宣布你們的公司幾天前已被「平靜公司」併購。你們當中若有人想要為「平靜公司」工作，可以於2013年8月31日前和我們人力資源經理安排面談。過了那個日期，我們便認定原員工沒有其他人對「平靜公司」職缺感興趣。

問題8：這段簡短談話的目的是？
A. 報告公司的新轉變。
B. 帶新的執行長參觀分公司。
C. 介紹新的經理。
D. 減低人力資源成本。

答案：A

問題9：這個公司剛發生了什麼事？
A. 公司雇用了新員工。
B. 公司發表了新產品。
C. 公司被「平靜公司」併購。
D. 公司設立了新的分公司。

答案：C

8.

女：筆記型電腦國際展將於波士頓舉行，我還在徵求一位員工和我還有我的口譯員一起前往。任何自認合格的人都可以向我提出申請。基本英文能力即可，因為如同我剛提到的，我們會有一個語言專員隨行。你們可能已聽說過了，像這樣的出差會很累人。這次出差的人可以於返台後馬上放一兩天的假。

問題10：這段簡短談話的主要訊息為何？
A. 近幾年來的年度銷售量。
B. 到國外出差的機會。
C. 下個月要參觀的城市。
D. 下個月要拜訪的客戶。

答案：B

問題11：下列關於員工的敘述何者為真？
A. 大部分員工去過波士頓出差。
B. 大部分員工喜歡這次出差，因為這樣就可以練習英文。
C. 大部分員工可能知道這次出差會很累人。

D. 大部分員工搶著想得到這個出國機會。

答案：C

問題12：這段簡短談話的結論最有可能為何？
A. 沒有人會參加這次出差。
B. 這次出差的人可以放幾天的假。
C. 公司不會再有這樣的出差。
D. 這次出差的人可以獲得一些錢。

答案：B

9.

女：詹姆士，我真的很喜歡你的簡報，非常中肯而且易了解。據我所知，這是你第一次用英文作簡報，整體而言，你的表現非常良好。或許下次你可以考慮使用一些圖表，因為視覺意象可以吸引更多的觀眾。像是這樣的簡報，或許你可以用標示出各洲銷售量的圓餅圖。

問題13：這裡在討論的主題為何？
A. 這位先生的英文理解能力。
B. 這女士的商業簡報。

C. 這位先生的第一次英文簡報。

D. 這女士的良好圖表與數據。

答案：C

問題14：這女士喜歡這位先生簡報的哪一部分？

A. 中肯而明白。

B. 附有圖表和數據。

C. 內容資訊別無僅有。

D. 有創意且不易被抄襲。

答案：A

問題15：這女士建議這位先生下次簡報怎麼做？

A. 縮短簡報長度。

B. 引用名人佳句。

C. 使用肢體語言。

D. 使用有數據的圖表。

答案：D

第二部份： 談話

本部份共 10 題。題目播放前將各有 30 秒的時間瀏覽圖表及新聞標題。每題播出一遍。

第 16 到 20 題為關於圖表上顯示某公司男性員工年收入相對於女性員工年收入的問題；每題請聽光碟放音機播出的問題並參考圖表後，選出正確答案。

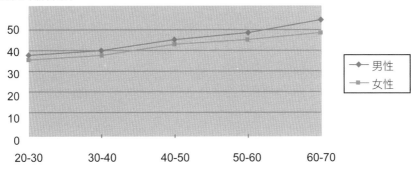

16. 這圖表代表什麼？
A. 員工的高收入和於公司的長年服務。
B. 經理角色和公司員工的年紀。
C. 年紀和所託付的不同任務之間的關係。
D. 公司不同年紀的男性和女性員工之年收入。

答案：D

17. 這家公司的員工可能幾歲退休？
A. 70

B. 65

C. 60

D. 55

答案：A

18. 這家公司的員工薪水和年紀有什麼關係？

A. 年紀和薪水之間沒有關係。

B. 年紀越高，薪水可能越高。

C. 年紀越高，工作就越輕鬆。

D. 薪水越高，第二年就越難獲得加薪。

答案：B

19. 下列關於男性和女性員工年收入的敘述何者為真？

A. 大部分女性員工對薪水感到不滿意。

B. 男性員工較有效率，所以薪水較高。

C. 男性和女性員工於公司裡一定擔任不同職務。

D. 普遍來說，男性員工的薪水較他們的女性同事來得高。

答案：D

20. 下列何者為員工年收入相對於年紀之變化的最佳敘述？

A. 穩定且持續的成長。

B. 緩慢的漸減。

C. 完全沒有增加。

D. 最終降到最低點。

答案：A

第 21 到 25 題為五篇新聞報導；每題請聽光碟放音機播出的新聞報導後, 從試題冊上 7 個選項中選出對應的標題。

21. 每年都有成千上萬的學生想要出國留學，但是並非所有學生都有充裕資金來付學費和海外生活開銷。現在越來越多的銀行想要進入留學生貸款的市場。這些銀行正考慮要延長年紀限制，好讓更多想要出國留學的人有機會貸款。教育部正在謹慎審核這些銀行的提案。

答案：B

22. 至今四十萬以上的人已經使用過台北微笑單車，其中包括本地人和國際觀光客。大部分的人對於前三十分鐘免費騎車的制度感到滿意；有些人抱怨要還微笑單車的時候找不到位置停車。還有人將微笑單車騎到太遠的地方而被罰款。整體而言，幾乎所有微笑單車的使用者都認為他們會盡可能使用微笑單車。

答案：E

23. 木材建築已經越來越受現代建築師的喜愛。這樣的綠建築的建築費用通常牽涉到伴隨而來的太陽能光板和水資源回收的設備。長遠來說，要維護這樣的建築其實較省錢。北投市立圖書館即是這類木材建築的成功例子。它獲得了國際肯定，吸引了許多參觀者。大部分設計綠建築的建築師認同與自然和諧共處的理念。

答案：A

24. 資源回收再製的產品並不少見，但是你看過用舊腳踏車零件所製成的產品嗎？就像世上所有其他東西，腳踏車的使用期限是有限的。無可避免地，主人必須要看到心愛的腳踏車進入垃圾堆積場。因此，一位腳踏車商店的主人想出了一個回收舊腳踏車來製作普通日常用品，像是桌子、椅子、櫥子的主意。這個點子很快於世界其他地方散播開來，現在很多腳踏車專家正跟上這股潮流。

答案：D

25. 很多青少年會犯罪是因為他們從前被虐待過。今年一月，有關當局成立許多新工作坊來幫助這些年輕人。有些犯罪的青少年本性不會很暴力，他們會接受建議去做些手工藝品，還有其他像是香皂

的產品。在像這樣的庇護工場裡,他們可以重新獲得自尊,同時他們手工產品所換來的錢可以讓他們支付基本生活開銷。這樣的情況對剛從青少年戒護所出來的年輕男女是雙贏的局面。

答案:G

A. 木製建築有益於環保。

B. 越來越多的銀行想要經營學生貸款。

C. 有關當局在重新思考都市更新。

D. 用舊腳踏車零件所製成的資源回收產品

E. 本地人和觀光客都喜歡微笑單車

F. 外籍建築師在台灣的機會

G. 受虐青少年的工作坊

第三部份: 長篇對話與談話

本部份包括一段長篇談話與一段對話,每段談話或對話播出一遍。每段談話或對話前有45秒的時間閱讀五個問題,聽完談話或對話後,會有一分鐘的答題時間,每題請從 A、B、C、D 四個選項中選出正確答案。

男:「下星期我們將參加於西雅圖舉行的國際照明產品與科技展。

從前像這樣的國際展覽顯示，大部分外國公司特別對我們的兩個領域感興趣：第一，設計獨特的LED燈瓦，特徵為內建照明、特薄、輕巧、高效能。第二個為我們公司吸引來眾多參觀者的地方是辦公室照明產品。你們大多曾參與並對我們屢屢獲獎的LED照明設計產品的研發過程貢獻良多。現在是你們對國際專家和消費者光榮展示你們神奇產品的時機。仔細研究我們這次參展型錄上的所有產品，因為你們很可能常會被問及並非是你們所設計的照明產品。我期待你們在任何時間都能回答任何問題。你們團員之間應該互相支持，尤其是在國外。我對你們在這個產業的英語溝通能力毫不懷疑，但是我仍然建議你們從今天起每天多聽英語新聞廣播來增強你們的語言能力。我對你們所有人深具信心，同時我保證你們會從這次經驗中學到很多東西，並由這次在美國的活動所將認識的商業夥伴獲益良多。」

26. 這位演說者的談話主旨是什麼？
A. 研究資金和獎學金。
B. 一個國際照明展覽。
C. 設計與生活方式。
D. 工業革命。

答案：B

27. 這些聽眾最可能為什麼人？
A. 不同照明公司的執行長。
B. LED照明產品的設計師。

C. LED照明產品工廠的製造商。

D. LED照明裝置的銷售人員。

答案：B

28. 這位演説者期待他的聽眾於參展前做什麼？

A. 與人交際。

B. 閱讀商務通訊。

C. 研讀型錄。

D. 訂機票。

答案：C

29. 在這段談話中，「增強」和下列何者的意思最相近？

A. 聆聽。

B. 使優美。

C. 扶養。

D. 明白。

答案：B

30. 這位演説者的語調如何？

A. 不情願的。

B. 高傲的。

C. 鼓勵的。

D. 同情的。

答案：C

經理：傑森，這位是英國來的安。安，這位是傑森，他是台灣關於經濟議題的專家。安剛結束於台東的市場調查之行。我想請你們兩位交換一下關於我們產品在東台灣行銷策略的意見。

傑森：安，很高興認識妳。妳何不先告訴我們妳對台東市場的觀察呢？

安：我在台東七天之行中，拜訪了我們許多不同巧克力產品和其他甜點的潛在零售商。除此之外，我和主要超級市場所有人開過會，聽取了他們的意見和回饋。

傑森：我們的英國甜點於台東的未來看來如何？

安：我們巧克力和其他甜點未來看來非常樂觀。雖然消費者抱怨西式食品的價錢高漲，例如潛艇堡，但是他們仍然繼續作忠實顧客。既然像潛艇堡那樣的西方品牌，價錢漲了那麼高仍然能在台東獲利，我們的精緻產品現在當然能夠進入市場。事實上，那裡大部分人對大多西方點心的品質和聲譽深具信心。

傑森：就潛艇堡的例子來說，它的行銷策略花了有一段時間才奏效。其他西方速食連鎖店也在媒體廣告投下巨資。何以見得像我們這樣的英國品牌能在東台灣這個新市場贏得顧客呢？

安：想必你們都認為我們的英國品牌在世界上聲譽優良，我們於英國國內市場佔有率領先各家。我們絕不可低估那裡居民的購買力。

傑森：妳剛所説的和我於媒體所觀察到的很相近。謝謝妳和我們分享妳的看法。

經理：這樣的話，我想我們很快可以於東部市場預見我們的產品。

31. 這位經理想要傑森與安討論什麼主題？
A. 於台東購買超級市場。
B. 參觀台東的巧克力工廠。
C. 他們產品於台東的行銷。
D. 於台東成立分公司。

答案：C

32. 安認為他們產品的前景如何？
A. 有希望的。
B. 倒退的。
C. 衰弱的。

D. 悲慘的。

答案：A

33. 為什麼安把台東的潛艇堡和他們的產品作比較？
A. 他們都有許多顧客。
B. 他們都才剛漲價。
C. 他們都曾一度流行。
D. 他們都是西方品牌。

答案：D

34. 為什麼傑森同意安的看法？
A. 最近的銷售量反映此結果。
B. 這和他的觀察相符合。
C. 這符合行銷策略。
D. 英國國內市場顯示出此點。

答案：B

35. 這個討論的結論為何？
A. 他們會在連鎖商店上投資大筆金錢。
B. 他們的巧克力會在美國上市。
C. 他們會在台東做更多的市場調查。
D. 他們的產品很快就會在東台灣上市。

答案：D

閱讀能力測驗

第一部份：圖表、書信、短文

本部份包括圖表及數篇短文。每個圖表及每篇短文後有二至四個相關問題，每題後有四個選項，請根據圖表及短文提供的線索，由試題冊上 A、B、C、D 四個選項中選出最適合者為答案。請在答案紙上找到對應題號塗黑作答。

（1）

答案：1.（B）　　2.（D）　　3.（C）

本文翻譯：

顧客滿意度調查表

為了確保我們提供的是最優質的服務，我們想要請您填寫以下的意見調查表，感謝您的幫忙。您的個人資料只會為渡假旅行社工作人員所使用。

基本資料

姓名：	溫蒂·張
公司：	京站購物中心
電話號碼：(02) 2367-3325	手機號碼：0942-553-256
電子郵件：	Wendyc0110@hotmail.com
最近您與我們聯絡的日期？	2013年 6月15日

您對我們整體的滿意度如何？

___ 極度不滿意

✓ 略為不滿意

___ 無意見

___ 略為滿意

___ 極度滿意

請為我們以下各項服務品質評分。

	極差	欠佳	普通	尚可	優良
員工的知識	____	✓	____	____	____
員工的熱誠	____	✓	____	____	____
行程選擇範圍	____	____	✓	____	____
旅遊安排	____	____	✓	____	____
導遊的服務	____	✓	____	____	____

意見欄：

台灣導遊的英文能力太差，因為他的英語溝通技巧欠佳，造成了許多誤會狀況，行程安排因此有待改善。
所選的餐廳和旅館尚可。

您還會再參加我們旅遊團嗎？

__ 非常不可能

✓ 有點不可能

__ 無意見

__ 有點可能

__ 非常可能

您會介紹我們給您的朋友或熟人嗎？

✓ 非常不可能

__ 有點不可能

__ 無意見

__ 有點可能

__ 非常可能

您的意見對我們極為重要。感謝您的寶貴時間。

《字彙與片語》

survey　調查表

questionnaire　意見調查表

range　範圍

問題：

1. 這問卷的主要目的是什麼？

A. 找出他們顧客的來源。

B. 得到顧客的意見。

C. 得知他們顧客薪水高低。

D. 雇用新員工。

2. 這位顧客為何不喜歡那位台灣導遊的服務？

A. 他欠缺知識。

B. 他不夠熱心幫忙。

C. 他沒有將旅程安排妥當。

D. 他的英語溝通能力欠佳。

3. 以下何者不是這位顧客的意見？

A. 這位顧客對導遊不滿意。

B. 這位顧客不會再回到這家旅行社。

C. 這位顧客抱怨餐廳和旅館。

D. 旅行社的那位台灣導遊需要增強英文能力。

(2)

答案：4.（B）　　5.（D）　　6.（A）　　7.（B）

本文翻譯：

實習機會

我們現在正在尋找一位學校圖書館員的實習生，任職日期從2013年9月1日開始。三個月實習結束後有機會成為學校正職圖書館員。我們於週末提供特別的訓練以及工作坊，實習生的薪水為每小時115元。

137

應徵者必須擁有圖書館學和／或資訊管理科學學位。教育背景對於獲得這個職缺有幫助，但並非必備條件。於學校環境中具有耐心、服務熱誠，以及認真工作的精神，是適合這份工作者的理想特質。

工作職責包括：

—— 與學校教師合作
—— 協助學生搜尋圖書館資訊
—— 提倡使用學習科技
—— 收集並分析數據以改善教學

請於2013年七月31日將您的申請書送交給我們，2013年八月31日前，我們會於學校官網公布結果。

潔西卡・林
人力資源部門主管
八德高級中學
電話：(02)2751 2181轉139
電子信箱：jessicalin@sunshine.com

《字彙與片語》
    internship　實習
    applicant　申請者；求職者

collaborate　合作

human resources　人力資源

問題：

4. 這告示的主要目的為何？

A. 編纂資料庫。

B. 徵求實習生。

C. 獲得優良叢書。

D. 為工作坊作廣告。

5. 這實習時期結束於何時？

A. 九月一日。

B. 八月底。

C. 九月底。

D. 十一月底。

6. 以下何者非申請這個實習機會的必要條件？

A. 教育背景。

B. 圖書館學。

C. 資料庫技能。

D. 高中畢業文憑。

7. 這工作描述概括大意是

A. 培訓教師。

B. 協助圖書館讀者。

C. 建立學生資料庫。

D. 於人力資源部門工作。

(3)

答案：8. (B)　　9. (C)　　10. (D)　　11. (C)

本文翻譯：

寄件者：愛麗絲・王

收件者：湯姆・布朗

主旨：《台北故事》的版權

日期：2013年六月18日　星期二　上午9：18：11

布朗先生：

謝謝您對我們張瑪莉所著之書《台北故事》感興趣。幾天後這本書
就會寄達您的著作版權代理公司。
既然我們還沒有合作過，請提供曾經和您合作過之至少兩家公司的
推薦人。請見附件中版權合作的建議方案。請告知我們這本書於您

的國家上市的特定條件，我們才好依此設定版權費用。如果您想要
變更或修改任何事項，請讓我知道。

我們樂意提供更多英國讀者會感興趣的書籍，歡迎您參觀我們出版
社的網站www.sunshine.com.tw。請點選螢幕最左側的目錄，那兒
有更多關於我們書籍的資訊。

如果您有其他問題，歡迎隨時聯絡我。

順頌商祺

_____

愛麗絲・王
國際版權主任
陽光出版社
電話：2989-6899轉219
電子信箱：alicewang@sunshine.com

_____

《字彙與片語》

　　copyright　版權

　　publishing house　出版社

　　catalogue　目錄

問題：

8. 王小姐為何寫這封電子郵件？

A. 為了買下某本書的版權。

B. 為了請代理商賣某本書的版權。

C. 為了請代理商寄給她更多書。

D. 為了要對代理商抱怨。

9. 出版社請代理商提出幾個推薦人？

A. 不需要。

B. 只要一個。

C. 兩個以上。

D. 兩個以下。

10. 附件最有可能是什麼？

A. 廣告。

B. 目錄。

C. 使用手冊。

D. 合約。

11. 關於這封電子郵件何者為非？

A. 著作版權代理商對於台灣的書感興趣。

B. 王小姐想要將台灣的書賣給英國的讀者。

C. 這家出版社和這代理商從前合作過。

D. 他們將會開始討論版權的條件。

(4)

答案：12. (B)　　13. (C)　　14. (C)

本文翻譯：

致所有員工的通告

2013年7月10日

為了確保我們辦公室全面禁菸，2013年7月31日開始我們將推行關於吸菸問題的新法規。吸菸同仁不能再於咖啡間吸菸，替代方案是他們必須要到我們小廚房外的陽台吸菸。於辦公室或是大樓內其他空間吸菸的人將會受到懲罰。於2013年8月中第一次違規的人會被警告一次，第二次違規的人會被罰五佰元台幣。9月1日之後，將不會給予任何警告，每次違規的罰金為一仟元台幣。

我們祝您健康、長壽！

亞歷山大・史瓦茲
亞洲區總經理
台灣賓士

電話：886-2-27512556轉19

電子信箱：alexschwarz@bmw.com

《字彙與片語》

regulation　規定

penalty　懲罰

offense　違反規定

warning　警告

問題：

12.　這位總經理為何要寫這張通告？

A.　為了要吸引員工。

B.　為了要宣布新規定。

C.　要叫吸菸的員工辭職。

D.　要員工一個月後戒菸。

13.　如果某人要吸菸的話，可以去哪裡？

A.　咖啡間。

B.　廁所。

C.　陽台。

D.　廚房。

14. 如果某人於九月第一次吸菸被發現的話，會被罰多少錢？

A. 零元。

B. 五佰元。

C. 一仟元。

D. 只有一次警告。

(5)

答案：15. (B)　　16. (D)　　17. (C)

本文翻譯：

太極活動時間表

時間	活動
09:30 至 10:00	報名 & 付報名費
10:00 至 10:20	敘舊時間
10:20 至 10:40	頒獎
10:40 至 11:00	演講
11:00 至 12:00	太極運動表演
12:00 至 13:30	卡拉OK、午餐
13:30 至 13:50	領獎 & 活動結束

《字彙與片語》

    timetable　時間表

    membership fee　會員費

    catch up　敘舊

    present awards　頒獎

問題：

15.　這時間表的目的為何？

A.　安排老闆的行程

B.　宣布此活動的節目表

C.　賣運動產品

D.　籌備募款聚會

16.　誰最可能收到這時間表？

A.　唱歌選手

B.　英文測驗考生

C.　運動產品廠商

D.　太極運動會員

17. 演講的主題可能為何？

A. 聘僱私人教練

B. 於健身中心健身

C. 太極與健康

D. 歌唱與其益處

第二部份：長篇文章

（一）本部份包括兩篇文章，每篇文章分成五個段落。請從方框內的六個句子中，選出最符合每個段落大意的句子。

（1）

答案：18. (F)　　19. (E)　　20. (D)　　21. (A)　　22. (C)

本文翻譯：

A. 關於身心障礙方面的議題已經有很大的進展。

B. 大部分的身心障礙者不願意找工作。

C. 身心障礙者的工作機會可望改善。

D. 很多身心障礙者面臨財務困難以及支持設備的欠缺。

E. 大部分的雇主不願意給身心障礙者工作機會。

F. 身心障礙求職者於求職時面臨巨大的障礙。

在台灣身心障礙者的就業處境

18. 雖然政府政府推行了一些宣導活動，但是身心障礙者的就業處境仍然有待改善。身心障礙求職者於求職時面臨想像不到的偏見與無比的困難，尤其是在目前經濟不穩定的時候。

19. 按照現行法規，私人企業規模超過67人依法必須要雇用1%的身心障礙員工；如果員工人數為67人，按規定至少一人必須為身心障礙者。政府機關超過34人，依法必須要雇用3%的身心障礙員工。然而，大部分的雇主不願意雇用身心障礙求職者，他們寧願繳錢給一個基金會，讓願意雇用超額的身心障礙員工的公司受惠。即使是雇用身心障礙員工的企業裡，同工不同酬的歧視現象也仍然普遍。

20. 身心障礙者的平均薪資遠低於全國平均薪資，而且大都遠低於最低薪資，這代表了大多數的身心障礙者必須要在金錢上依賴他們的家人，才能收支平衡。很多身心障礙求職者經常沒有辦法找到適合的工作，為了生計必須要做任何能找到的工作。大部分的工作場所沒有身心障礙員工所需的基本設備，例如輪椅族所需的設備。

21. 相較於以往，身心障礙者之健康保險和教育方面有所進步。目前幾乎所有身心障礙者都被納入全民健康保險系統中，而且越來越多的身心障礙學生能透過政府特別教育課程，進入大學就讀。

22. 以大學為首,各級學校日益增多,身心障礙學生目前有越來越多的機會,得以進入他們所需的學習機構就讀。隨著社會大眾對身心障礙者的觀感逐漸改變,身心障礙者的就業處境可望逐漸且持續獲得改善。

《字彙與片語》

    campaign　宣導活動

    prejudice　偏見

    tremendous　無比的

    reluctant　不願意的

    adequately　足夠地

    facility　設備

    perception　觀點

(2)

答案:23.(B)　　24.(F)　　25.(D)　　26.(E)　　27.(A)

本文翻譯:

A. 原住民設計師的成品是他們跨文化的溝通方式。

B. 最近原住民文創產品在市場上非常成功。

C. 要鑑定原住民文創產品的真偽不容易。

D. 原住民文創產品帶來了就業機會。

E. 原住民文創產品很獨特，因此大受市場歡迎。

F. 原住民產品提昇了原住民的自尊，也改善了社會大眾對原住民文化的觀感。

原住民文創產品

23. 最近帶有原住民特色和意象的設計產品成了主流顧客的寵兒，大部分產品屬於文化創意產業，從帶有部落圖騰的桌燈到手織布袋，這些都是原住民設計師與商業團體和政府決策者共同努力的結果。

24. 一般來説，台灣文化在國際間的能見度很低，更不用説是原住民文化。帶有原住民特色的現代設計產品於某種程度上增進了大眾對當代原住民文化的認知，原住民的自尊因而得以提昇。這些結合藝術和產品的文化層面改善了原住民文化於社會大眾心中的形象。

25. 原住民的就業處境一向平均較其他求職者黯淡，很多年輕原住民來到大城市想找理想工作，只有極少數幸運者能找到薪水還算可以的工作，於都市叢林中倖存下來。現在有原住民文化產品工作坊，許多年輕原住民能在那裡找到實習機會，學習有用的技能，像是木雕或桌椅設計製作。從事與其部落傳統相關的工作帶給他們自

身極大的成就感。

26. 原住民文化產品的獨特性於目前市場具有競爭優勢，像這樣古老部落文化的再生，為工業設計帶來了活力，也吸引了原住民與非原住民顧客。無論在台灣和國外，原住民設計產品都引起極大的迴響，包含有國際藝術收藏家和購買紀念品的觀光客。

27. 像這樣的產品可作為文化創意產業的好例子。原住民設計師帶來他們文化的復興，至少成功將他們文化符號與意象轉換為引起顧客興趣的現代產品。藉著他們的作品，他們開啟了跨文化的溝通，讓他們具體的作品為他們無形的原住民文化發聲。（改編自《台灣光華雜誌》，2011年10月）

《字彙與片語》

> trendy　流行的
>
> mainstream　主流的
>
> tribal totem　部落圖騰
>
> decision-maker　決策者
>
> contemporary　當代的
>
> achievement　成就感
>
> competitive edge　競爭優勢
>
> revival　復興
>
> cultural symbol　文化符號

initiate 開始

cross-communication 跨文化的溝通

（二）本部份包括兩篇文章，每篇文章各有四個及六個空格，請由文章下方方框內提供的選項中，選出正確的句子放回文章空格。每篇文章各標示一句例答供參考。選項中有一個句子不會用到。

(1)

答案：28.（C）　　29.（E）　　30.（D）　　31.（A）

本文翻譯：

改編小說為電影

很多經常上電影院的人可能已經注意到，改編小說為電影於電影業早已流行許久。

2012年的英國喜劇片《金盞花大酒店》為這類成功的賣座電影之一，改編自2004年小說《那些蠢事》。另一個例子是改編自同名小說的《少年Pi 的奇幻漂流》。（28）_____.

文學專家傾向於對劇本的品質缺乏信心。（29）_____. 要確保原著小說的原來風貌得以保留，需要有優良的編劇技巧。許多的電影改編座談會和工作坊便為了想成為傑出編劇的人而應運而生。

大部分的英文老師會建議他們的學生先閱讀原著小說,然後再去看電影。(30)_____. 畢竟很少人能夠有那麼多寶貴時間既看書又看電影,更不用說是比較兩者當中的差異。

出版界對於大眾閱讀興趣似乎有所提昇而感到高興。(31)_____. 投資者看到了潛在的市場,願意贊助年輕的新手編劇。總而言之,對於出版業和電影業來說,這都是雙贏的局面。

可選擇的選項:

A. 看完改編自小說的電影,很多人決定去買暢銷小說。

B. 大部分看電影的人對於改編自有名小說的片子沒有多大興趣。

C. 結果這部電影非常轟動,並且提昇了台灣的形象。

D. 然而,很多人選擇去看電影,而不讀原著小說。

E. 換句話說,他們質疑電影是否保留了原著小說的精髓。

《字彙與片語》

adapt 改編

blockbuster 賣座電影

screenplay 劇本

screenwriting 編劇

win-win situation 雙贏的局面

(2)

答案：32. (B)　　33. (C)　　34. (E)　　35. (D)

本文翻譯：

台灣的觀光醫療

觀光醫療套裝行程最近非常流行。（32）＿＿＿＿＿＿．　這些外國旅客為了各類醫療服務來到台灣，包括健康檢查、牙醫服務、整型醫美等等，同時也能享受台灣美景。

（33）＿＿＿＿＿＿．　台灣高水準的醫師團隊久享盛名，大部分醫師會說英語，有些也會說日語。到目前為止，台灣觀光醫療吸引到的大多是說中文的病患，像是陸客以及海外華人。漸漸地，美國和澳大利亞也派專家來台灣勘查台灣所提供的醫療服務品質。

另一個原因是台灣醫療費用非常合理。（34）＿＿＿＿＿＿．　醫療機構提供最新科技，保障病人的手術和檢驗既省時又省錢。病人可以將省下來的時間和金錢，用來享受觀光或購物，讓他們於台灣的旅程發揮最大價值。

台灣不只是觀光的最理想地點，同時也是療養的好去處。剛動過手術的病人需要徹底休息，而台灣各地遍佈具有療效的溫泉景點。慢性病症患者可以於台灣森林綠地獲得自然療效。一年四季裡，國際旅客都可以於這美麗島嶼上發現新和舊的醫療吸引力。

日益發達的觀光醫療帶來的新的機會和挑戰。許多醫院已經開始和

航空公司、旅館業者和渡假村合作，以規劃出可行的計畫來滿足觀光醫療旅客日益增多的需求。（35）_____.　據估計，30,000的工作機會可應運而生，大部分居民對觀光醫療的前景持正面的看法。

可選擇的選項：

A. 台灣醫師以治癒慢性病症聞名。

B. 台灣無疑是觀光醫療最佳目的地之一。

C. 一個顯著原因是台灣擁有世界級的醫師、醫院、醫療系統。

D. 移民局尚要處理突然激增的觀光醫療旅客帶來的問題。

E. 旅客可以極低的費用享受台灣如此傑出的醫療服務。

《字彙與片語》

　　cosmetic surgery　整型手術

　　reasonable　合理的

　　cutting-edge technology　最新科技

　　recuperation　療養

　　therapeutic　具有療效的

　　booming　日益發達的

史上最強
GEPT Pro
企業英檢一本就夠
Mastering the GEPT Pro
The General English Proficiency Test Professional

Chapter. 05

第二回
模擬試題

Mastering the GEPT Pro
The General English Proficiency Test
Professional

THE SECOND TEST

LISTENING COMPREHENSION

Part I: Conversations and Short Talks

In Part I, you will hear five conversations and four short talks. Each conversation and talk will be played just one time. After each conversation or talk, you will hear one to three comprehension questions. When you hear each question, read the four choices in your test booklet and choose the best answer to the question you have heard.

1.

W: I heard you are flying to Hong Kong this weekend again.

M: Yes, I'd like to talk to my clients about some details.

W: Do you know you can have a virtual meeting online?

M: I know what you mean, but it didn't work out well for me.

W: As long as you are willing to pay for the travel

expenses, I won't have any problem.

Question: What does the woman suggest the man do?

A. To fly to Hong Kong.

B. To talk to clients online.

C. To travel to other places.

D. To learn new computer skills.

2.

Track 28

M:　Do you know all products are 40% off here at this toy fair?

W: Does that include the toys from Japan?

M: Certainly. In fact, I just saw some Japanese toys sold at 50% off.

W: What a bargain! Can you take me to that section?

M: I'll show you the way.

Question: What are these two people mainly talking about?

A. The quality of the Japanese toys.

B. Where the toys are from.

C. The safety of Japanese toys.

D. The discounts of the toys at a fair.

3.

Track 29

W: John, do you know how to use PowerPoint?

M: Well, I've never learned how it works.

W: How come?

M: I guess I just haven't had any chance to do a presentation.

W: In that case, this Friday will be your first chance.

Question: Why hasn't John learned PowerPoint yet?

A. He hasn't had the opportunity to do so.

B. He prefers to let others run PowerPoint for him.

C. He does not feel at ease with any software.

D. He dislikes doing a presentation.

Track 30

4.

M: Do you know why Robert and Tom don't get along with each other?

W: Haven't you heard that they are fighting over the manager position?

M: It seems to be a tough competition.

W: You are probably the last person in this office to notice it.

M: Of course, I wouldn't want to have anything to do with the fierce game.

Question: What is the main problem between Robert and Tom?

A. They are in a competition for the manager position.

B. They are interested in the same female colleague.

C. They do not like each other's personalities.

D. They cannot agree with each other on several procedures.

5.

M: Judging from your previous experiences, you are really over-qualified.

W: What I like about this job is that I can work from home, and it is almost like a part-time job to me.

M: Why wouldn't you want to work in an office?

W: I have two small kids to look after, and most full-time jobs in the office simply don't suit me.

M: Why don't you send me the first few sketches?

Question: What makes the man consider the woman almost too good for this job?

A. Her sincere attitude.

B. Her outstanding graphic works.

C. Her creative ideas.

D. Her excellent work experiences.

6.

M: Many people ask which type of camera they should buy

when it comes to purchasing such a product. Take digital cameras for an example: They come in all models, sizes, features, and prices. To make a wise purchase, you should find out your exact needs and budget. One more important thing to pay attention to is that for a product like a digital camera, technology is developing at an astonishing speed. A digital camera bought 5 years ago might be considered an antique by today's standard. To help with your decision-making process, we provide you with our informative catalogs on the 1st of each month.

Question 6: What is the man trying to do here?
A. He is talking about the making of a camera.
B. He is explaining the history of digital cameras.
C. He is advertising the cameras of his company.
D. He is analyzing the components of a camera.

Question 7: What advice does the man give in the end?
A. Camera buyers can take a look at their monthly catalogs.
B. People should use digital cameras instead of traditional cameras.
C. The features of the latest camera are always the best.
D. People should buy a one-fit-all type of digital camera.

7.

W: This is Sue Wang, your personal financial advisor from ANZ Bank in Taipei. The day before yesterday you requested the personal loan application form, but the correct form was not available at that time. Now I can send the form you need to you at your convenience. This loan plan is only valid until Sept. 30, 2013. Please do call me back soon at (02) 2675-8942 extension 62. Thank you very much.

Question 8: Why does this woman leave a message on the answering machine?

A. To advertise a personal loan.

B. To check the credit card bills.

C. To deliver the loan application form.

D. To report the loan interest.

Question 9: What kind of loan did the client want to apply for?

A. Home loan.

B. Car loan.

C. Small business loan.

D. Personal loan.

8.

M： Since we launched the system of membership cards early this year, we expected the overall sales would rise by at least 7% by the end of June. The real performance from January to June has not been as good as we would like to see： It is only 4%. We hope that by the end of December this year, we can really profit from the memberships cards, and the sales increase will become double what we have seen within the first half of the year.

Question 10： What is the main topic of this short talk?
A. The membership cards and big sales.
B. The qualifications to apply for membership cards.
C. The membership cards and sales increase.
D. The benefits of membership cards.

Question 11： What does the speaker hope the system of membership cards can bring?
A. The membership card holders can receive bonuses.
B. As time goes by, more profit can be made from the system.
C. The membership cards cannot be used in another branch store.
D. The speaker thinks the system of membership cards is useless.

Question 12: What kind of sales increase does the speaker expect to see by the end of this year?

A. 7%

B. 14%

C. 4%

D. 8%

9.

M: I am the representative of the Teacher's Union, Chang Da-cheng. I want to thank those who came here because of my announcement of this peaceful demonstration on my Facebook page. We are here to campaign for the basic benefits of private teachers, namely, retirement pension. After postponing this strike from June 30 to July 31 and finally to August 31, I can only say that we have given the authority concerned plenty of chances to respond to our request. Unfortunately, we waited in vain. Now we are sitting peacefully in the Liberty Square on August 31, the day before many schools start a new academic year. As much as we wouldn't want to see it happen, we are forced to consider quitting teaching in the coming days if this serious issue is still left unanswered.

Question 13: How does the speaker mobilize the fellow teachers to join this strike?

A. Union's newsletter.

B. Teacher's Union.

C. Labor Agency.

D. Social media.

Question 14： When does this peaceful demonstration actually take place?

A. June 30.

B. July 31.

C. Aug. 31.

D. Sept. 30.

Question 15： What do these teachers campaign for?

A. Liberty.

B. More wages.

C. Pension.

D. Less workload.

Part II： Talks

There are ten questions in this part. Before listening to the recording, you will have 30 seconds to study the graph and read the headlines printed in the test booklet. Each

recording will be played just once.

For questions 16 to 20, you will hear five questions about the percentages of Taiwan's main exports partners on a graph. After you hear each question, choose the best answer to the question you have heard.

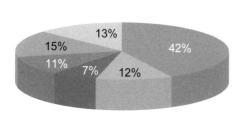

■ Mainland China& Hong Kong	42%	
■ USA	12%	
■ Japan	7%	
■ Europe	11%	
■ ASEAN countries	15%	
■ Other countries	13%	

16. What does this graph tell us about Taiwan's main export partners?

A. The development of each main export business.

B. The proportion of each main export partner in the total.

C. The future potentials of each main export partner.

D. The economy of each main export partner.

17. Which main export partner dominates Taiwan's exports

trading business?

A. Japan.

B. USA.

C. Mainland China & Hong Kong.

D. Europe.

18. According to this graph, which country in Northeastern Asia is Taiwan's largest export partner after China?

A. Malaysia.

B. Singapore.

C. Japan.

D. Indonesia.

19. Which country has about the same amount of export business with Taiwan as Europe?

A. China.

B. The United States.

C. Japan.

D. Hong Kong.

20. What is the percentage of the other countries which are not stated in the graph?

A. 11%

B. 12%

C. 13%

D. 14%

For questions 21 to 25, you will hear five news reports. After you hear each news report, choose the headline from the list that best matches the news report you have heard.

21. Without any sign or warning, the Kingdom English School closed suddenly. Last Friday evening most school children went to the language school as usual, only to find the school had closed permanently. Parents are now very upset because the tuition fees they paid probably will never be refunded. English schools like this are all private and the government regulations do not always apply to them. We were unable to contact the owners responsible for the Kingdom English School at this time.

22. When asked why they lie in the workplace, many office staff say that others lie first. It is a sad truth that most employees no longer trust those whom they work with and are above them. In order to secure their own benefits, they decide to adopt the strategy of lying, just like the rest of the team. In the long run, the foundation of trust is destroyed by the lies. If communication cannot

eliminate lies, it is not constructive communication at all. Liars in the workplace should think about the long-term effects of their lying.

Track
39

23. Dental Insurance started not long ago in the West, but in Taiwan few people have such insurance. The idea behind dental insurance is clear and simple enough: The high expenses of dental surgery services are similar to the treatments of other illnesses, and therefore the risks can be similarly managed. Whether the consumers in Taiwan will follow this new trend, it is still too early to tell. Most dentists, however, hope that their patients are properly insured so that they can provide their patients with the affordable medical services they need.

Track
40

24. Those who have been to Hualien recently may have noticed the increasing numbers of Bed-n-Breakfasts. Most of them are run by couples and some of the local owners are from indigenous backgrounds. They feature the local flavor in their interior designs and cuisines. Within a short period of time, these well-managed Bed-n-Breakfasts have attracted loyal customers who come back again and again. Although some locals worry about the impact of tourists on the area, most people are happy to see the boost in economy.

25. Online shopping is common nowadays, but have you heard of online grocery shopping? A person shops for you at the supermarket on a regular basis and then delivers the groceries to your door. Many online companies are evaluating the possibility of providing such service. Their main concern is how to attract enough customers who will sign a yearly contract with them for such home delivery service. The responses of American and European office white collars are relatively high, but in Taiwan, most people seem to prefer doing shopping on their own.

A. Online Grocery Shopping Service

B. Bed-n-Breakfasts are Popular in Hualien

C. Insurance for Overseas Students

D. Office Staff Get Together to Shop Online

E. Dental Insurance is New in Taiwan

F. Kingdom English School Closed Suddenly Last Friday

G. Lies in the Workplace

Part III: Long Talk & Long Conversation

In Part III, you will hear one long talk and one long conversation. Each of them will be played only once. Before you listen to each talk or conversation, you will have 45 seconds to read the questions printed in the test booklet. After hearing the recording, you will have one minute to answer the questions. Choose the correct answer from the choices A, B, C, or D.

W: Today I would like draw your attention to the importance of law in the world of advertising business.

As you might have read in the recent newspaper, quite a few major firms of industrial design were caught in legal battles over the issue of copyrights. Such cases could have been avoided if the designers had paid more attention to intellectual property rights. This can apply to our advertising agency as well.

Whenever you are thinking about a slogan or a scene in one commercial, ask yourself or your team members:

Are they original slogans? Has it appeared in other commercials? Or more directly: Have I seen it somewhere else before? Have I subconsciously copied the creative idea from somebody else? If so, make sure you do ask the original writer or designer, if you could use their ideas with your own alterations. This is not merely an act of courtesy, it can indeed prevent you from ending up in the

law suits of plagiarism. There are people who think they could use or steal others' ideas in a foreign country and apply them directly in Taiwan. In this day and age, information travels far and fast on the Internet and other media, and such wrong doings often are caught immediately. Thus we often hear of foreign companies arriving in Taiwan and bringing law suits against Taiwanese firms. Huge amounts of money would thus be lost in providing the compensation, but the worst consequence for a Taiwanese firm is that their reputation would be damaged beyond repair, particularly internationally.

26. What is the main topic of this talk?
A. Creative thinking and design.
B. Sharing ideas and thoughts.
C. Creativity and industrial design.
D. Copyright and advertisement.

27. Which industry are the speaker and the listeners in?
A. Graphic design.
B. Advertisement.
C. Publishing.
D. Marketing.

28. What does the word "plagiarism" possibly mean in

this context?

A. Property invasion or illegal use.

B. False advertisement or fraud.

C. Unauthorized use or imitation.

D. Cooperation or brain drain.

29. What is the common mistake mentioned by the speaker?

A. Applying ideas from a company overseas without permission.

B. Analyzing the successful cases abroad and using their experiences.

C. Hiring foreign designers instead of Taiwanese talents.

D. Taking their products abroad without ever coming back.

30. What does the speaker find more damaging to the company than the penalties if plagiarism is caught?

A. The quality of the commercials.

B. The deals of the firm.

C. The clients of the advertisement.

D. The image of the company.

Track
43

M: "Welcome to Golden Phoenix Company on the last day of the International Laptop Exhibition in Taipei. How can I help you?"

W: "Could you please introduce some of the new models of

your company's laptops to me?"

M: "Sure. May I ask what your budget is about?"

W: "In fact, I have no idea of a reasonable price of a laptop, but my roommate got one laptop at 19,990 Taiwan Dollars. Do you have laptops in that price range?"

M: "Of course. Please take a look at this model, featuring wide screen and that one, very light in weight. Both of them cost 18,000 Taiwan Dollars."

W: "Can I get a discount? I am currently studying Chinese at National Normal University, and I have my American passport with me."

M: "We can give you 5% student discount, as long as you can show us your international student card."

W: "In that case, I'll take the left one with the pink cover."

M: "We understand that many students have financial restraint, so we offer installment plans for such a laptop purchase. Installment Plan A allows you to pay over 6 months, that is monthly 3000 Taiwan Dollars, and Installment Plan B, 12 months, 1500 Taiwan Dollars a month. There is absolutely no interest involved."

W: "I'd like to be on the Installment Plan B. Could I pay with my VISA credit card?"

M: "You are welcome to do so. Don't forget to show your international student card to our cashier."

W: "Can I take my new laptop home today or do I have to wait for somebody to deliver the laptop to my place?"

M: "You can have the new laptop right after signing the contract of installment plan B and the agreement of credit card payment."

31. Where does this conversation take place?

A. A co-op for students.

B. A computer hardware shop.

C. A conference of computer science.

D. An International Laptop Show.

32. What does the woman have to present in order to get a discount?

A. Valid passport.

B. Membership card.

C. International student card.

D. Driving license.

33. How much money is the woman going to pay monthly for her new laptop?

A. 1500 Taiwan Dollars.

B. 3000 Taiwan Dollars.

C. 6000 Taiwan Dollars.

D. 7500 Taiwan Dollars.

34. How is the woman going to pay for her new laptop?

A. In cash.

B. With a credit card.

C. Partly in cash and partly with a credit card.

D. With a debit card.

35. What does the woman have to do before taking her new laptop home?

A. Pay the first installment.

B. Sign the contracts.

C. Make a down payment.

D. Bargain on the price.

READING COMPREHENSION

Part One：Charts, Letters and Short Essays

In this part of the test, you will find charts and several passages. Each chart or passage is followed by two to four questions. You are to choose the BEST answer, A, B, C or D, to each question on the basis of the information provided in the chart or passage. Then, on your answer

sheet, find the number of the question and mark your
answer.

(1)

Job Interview Procedure

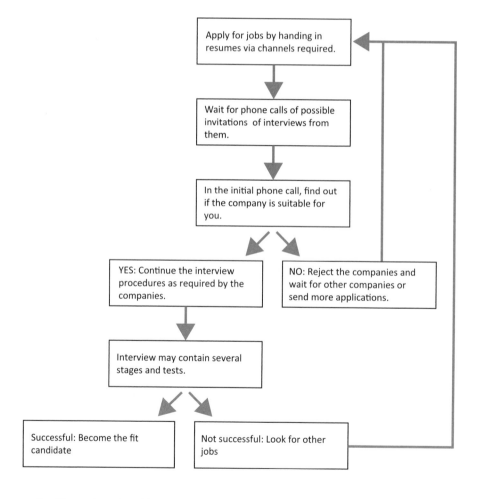

1. What is the flow chart designed for?
A. To do a business survey of companies.

B. To obtain information of human resources.

C. To demonstrate how to apply for work.

D. To know more about corporate culture.

2. What is recommended to do in the initial phone conversation?

A. To project a good image of oneself.

B. To get to know the human resource executive.

C. To try to get more information about the company.

D. To impress them with your profile.

3. Who will find this flow chart most useful?

A. Those who are job-hunting.

B. Those who run small businesses.

C. The customers who wish to complain to a company.

D. The managers who supervise a department.

4. Which statement about this flow chart is NOT true?

A. It shows a good procedure to find a job.

B. It tells us that interviews can be conducted more than once.

C. It guarantees a reliable solution to one's unemployment.

D. It is designed mainly for job-applicants.

(2)

From : Linda Chen

To : Judy Richardson

Subject : The watch repair

Date : Sat, June 29, 2013 10 : 09 : 54 a.m.

Dear Ms. Richardson,

Here I refer to the watch I purchased on April 15, 2013, with a one-year warranty period. The watch stopped one month after I bought it. Afterwards, I went to the watch retail shop where I bought the watch and was told that the battery had already run out. The clerk replaced the battery, but a couple days ago, the watch stopped again in spite of the new battery. To solve the technical problems inside, I then went to the watch shop and asked the clerk for help. He asked me to fill out the repair form and told me that he would have the watch sent to the department of technical support in your company. To my surprise, one week later, there was a new female clerk working in the watch shop and she could not find my form or data anywhere. The new female clerk could not help me

much, and that is why I am writing to you in customer service of the main office in Asia to seek help.

Please find the attachment of the scanned picture of the one-year warranty certificate.

Best Regards,

_____

Linda Chen

Tel : 2479-8931

Email : lindachen@yahoo.com.tw

_____

5. Why does Ms. Linda Chen write the e-mail?

A. To complain about the price of her watch.

B. To have a watch hand-made for her.

C. To say thanks for the service of the watch shop.

D. To enquire about the repair of her watch.

6. What did the clerk do to fix Linda's watch the first time?

A. He examined the watch thoroughly.

B. He replaced the battery in the watch.

C. He repaired the watch with somebody's help.

D. He gave Linda a completely new watch.

7. Who is possibly Ms. Judy Richardson?

A. A watch retail shop clerk.

B. A customer service supervisor.

C. A watch designer.

D. A watch repair technician.

(3)

Health packages for companies

In our leading Vitality Gym, we offer companies special-designed health packages, which include :

1. A Health check-up

2. Seminars on health issues

3. Weight loss programs

4. Customized sports classes and programs

5. Professional trainers for office workers

6. Professional evaluation in the end

With the above-mentioned services, we are confident that

we can help your staff members successfully manage their health. After the health check-up, we will offer specially designed training programs with our professional coaches to suit your staff's needs. Our trainers can motivate, monitor, and help your staff achieve the goals set up in the beginning. Please contact Mr. Chang for the early bird price.

8. What is the purpose of this short article?
A. To advertise a weight loss summer camp.
B. To campaign the importance of sport.
C. To attract customers to buy their sports packages.
D. To announce the opening of a new gym.

9. Which of the following is NOT offered in the package?
A. Sports coaches.
B. Training sessions.
C. Weight management.
D. Seminars on customer service.

10. What does the word "customized" most likely mean here?
A. It is based on traditional customs.
B. It is specially designed for customers.
C. It is related to souvenirs.

D. It is a kind of training facility.

11. Who is this advertisement most likely addressed to?
A. A trainee in a restaurant.
B. An Intern in a company.
C. A small business owner.
D. An accountant in a firm.

(4)

Taipei, August 21, 2013

Schedule of business trip to China

The schedule of our group business trip to Guangzhou, China, from Monday, September 2 to Saturday, September 7, 2013, has been decided as the following. If anyone has any suggestions, please do not hesitate to e-mail our secretary, Miss Huang, and she will pass them on to me. The flight and hotel accommodation are already booked, but if necessary, we can extend two more days maximum.

Day one Noon： Arrival at Star Hotel in Guangzhou
Dinner with executives from Goal Company

Day two Touring the manufacturing factory of computer chips

Day three Business meeting with suppliers to discuss and sign the contracts

Day four Visits to laptop retail shops

Day five Sightseeing

Day six Checking out of the hotel and catching return flight to Taiwan

If there is no feedback from any of you, I will assume that this schedule is acceptable. Thank you for your attention.

General Manager
Jack Pan

12. What sort of schedule is this?

A. A schedule for office routine.

B. A schedule for tasks to be done.

C. A schedule for a business tour.

D. A schedule for sightseeing in China.

13. When could be the latest day they return from Guangzhou to Taipei?

A. September 7, 2013.

B. September 9, 2013.

C. September 2, 2013.

D. It is not mentioned here.

14. What is NOT true about the person who wrote this notice?

A. He is a general manager.

B. He is announcing the schedule of a business trip.

C. He is the only person who will go on the trip.

D. He wants to hear others' opinions.

(5)

Places Where Orders Come from in 2012

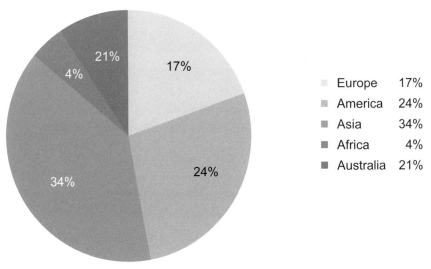

■ Europe 17%
■ America 24%
■ Asia 34%
■ Africa 4%
■ Australia 21%

15. What does this pie chart show us?

A. The proportions of where orders are from.

B. The percentages of goods made.

C. The destinations of business trips.

D. The preferences of products.

16. According to this pie chart, where do most orders come from?

A. Australia.

B. Asia.

C. Europe.

D. America.

17. Where is the pie chart most likely used?

A. In a concert hall.

B. In a business conference room.

C. In a train station.

D. In the international airport.

Part Two： Essays

Task I： Matching Summary Statements

In each box, five of the six statements are paragraph summaries for the text that follows. Match the statements with the paragraphs. Choose one of the statements from the list (A-F) for each paragraph. One of the summary sentences in each box will not be used.

(1)

A. Only a very small portion of all products in organic food stores are truly organic.

B. It is believed that organic food customers in Taiwan will increase.

C. Why are the prices so high?

D. Organic food stores have a longer history in Taiwan than in America.

E. Generally speaking, there are four kinds of organic food stores here.

F. The image of organic food stores is very positive in Taiwan.

Organic Food Stores in Taiwan

18. More and more people shop in organic food stores these days in Taiwan. Organic food stores often claim all their products come directly from the farm to the market. Some offer bread right from the oven and freshly made juice for customers to taste; others even provide cooking classes and seminars on health issues.

19. If we analyze the organic food stores, also called health food stores, we can find they come in four types, depending on the various organizers: doctors, religious leaders, survivors of serious illnesses, and environmentalists promoting organic lifestyles. They all believe in the importance of nutrition.

20. Despite all their good intentions, not all their products are truly organic; in fact, only 20-30% of the average overall sales can be called "organic" in such a store. It might seem deceiving, but the truth is that

in Taiwan, most organic food stores have to sell other products in order to survive.

21. Customers might ask : Why is organic food so expensive? Generally speaking, organic food costs more than non-organic food. It is especially true in Taiwan. Experts believe that it is because in Taiwan the organic food industry developed much later than in some other countries. Production technology and marketing channels therefore are not as mature as in most western countries.

22. Many customers are aware of the advantages of organic food, but due to the high prices, they are not able to shop in organic food stores as often as they wish. It is hoped that with the development of production technology and marketing, the prices of organic food will become more and more acceptable to most customers in Taiwan.

(2)

A. With risks involved, self-employment brings a higher income.

B. Many self-employees become unemployed in the end.

C. Quite a few self-employed workers complain about loneliness.

D. Whether one should be self-employed depends on the nature of one's work.

E. Not all people have what it takes to be a good self-employee and an entrepreneur.

Are you suitable for self-employment?

23. Many people associate self-employment with entrepreneurship. The idea of being able to run one's own business and to be one's own boss appeals to many people who enter the job market, particularly the younger generation. Before deciding to work on one's own, one should reflect on one's own personal characteristics. Not all people can handle risks very well; self-discipline is another criterion needed to push oneself to work in social isolation.

24. The average incomes of the self-employed are lower than that of traditional employees in the early stages, but, as time goes by, their incomes surpass what the traditional workers on average earn. Over all, the self-employed do make more money than those who work for others. Naturally, self-employment involves more decision-

making and risks. Entrepreneurship is called for in managing one's small business.

25. The freedom of being able to work at one's own pace, in one's own space sounds all so attractive, but the lack of social contacts renders often sense of loneliness. Isolation from others means being able to not to be disturbed by annoying colleagues, but the lack of social interaction is not healthy in the long run. Some rent and share office-space with others to solve the issue.

26. Besides, it is wise to take the very nature of one's work into consideration. Writers, translators and free-lancers are appropriate for self-employment. On the other hand, if one's work relies on constantly brainstorming with team members, it might not be smart to adopt self-employment.

Task II: Choosing Correct Sentences

Ten sentences have been removed from the two texts that follow. From the sentences in the boxes at the bottom of the pages, choose the sentence that best fits in each

gap. One of the missing sentences for each text has been correctly filled in as an example. One of the sentences in each box will not be used.

(1)

Leadership

Within an organization like a commercial company, managerial roles from chief executives to small departmental supervisors all require the ability to lead a team, generally called "leadership." Workshops and books on leadership are in high demand, and new theories and practices emerge almost every day. Generally speaking, there are four essential qualities that make up good leadership skills.

Strength：(27)_____. Of course, beside social skills, it is essential to have a wide knowledge of the company and the particular trade of business.

Warmth：Warmth often comes with empathy, familiarity and sometimes, charisma. (28)_____. In many Taiwanese companies, employers are often perceived as a parent figure. Some people even use the term "Machiavellian" to describe those leaders, who are feared and loved at the same time.

Prioritization: All leading figures have to prioritize tasks and agendas very well and organize precious resources like time and money accordingly. In the present time full of economic uncertainty, it takes a wise leader to decide when to take action and when to find the stop loss point. (29)_____.

Unity: (30)_____. Each member should be made aware of his or her duty in contributing to achieving those goals. A team leader should be well aware of the loyalty of the team members and deal efficiently with those who will tear at the unity of a team.

Strength, warmth, prioritization and unity characterize outstanding leaders in the business world. They may seem simple, but a novice leader might find it quite hard to master them.

ANSWERS to choose from:

A. Effective prioritization is the essential skill one needs to make the most of the efforts of one's team.

B. To make sure that a team is fully united, clear common goals should be established.

C. Rewarding the employees for well-done work is highly recommended.

D. Nice personality usually characterizes an excellent supervisor in a firm.

E. A competent leader in a company setting should have, in the first place, strength to lead the team.

(2)

The Pros and Cons of eBooks

Like all technological advances in other fields, eBooks have made a great impact on the way we read nowadays. Many readers have not anticipated such a modern form of reading and are still observing the market. Others, especially young people, are embracing and enjoying the advantages of eBooks.

Here are some major advantages that most eBook readers would tell their friends without hesitation:

First, compared to traditional paper books, eBooks offer a much lighter way to transport reading materials. All a reader has to do is purchase an electronic device, which often connects to the Internet and related services. (31)_____.

Second, the fact that eBooks use no paper is environmentally friendly. (32)_____. Knowing that no trees were sacrificed because of the products certainly gives them a clear conscience.

Last but not least, eBooks contain multi-media and electronic texts, which are easy to search, highlight, save, and even edit. Senior readers can enlarge the font size easily for their far-sightedness. Sharing electronic files with others becomes much easier than before.

The issue of eyesight can be a disadvantage as well. Many people have suffered problems of eyesight due to prolonged hours of computer usage. Reading devices on the market now are even smaller than the ordinary laptop screens. (33)_____.

For the publishing industry, piracy is a subsequent disaster that comes with the very nature of eBooks. (34)_____. Many publishing companies are thus unwilling to launch eBooks at this stage.

Quite a few publishing houses are confident about traditional paper books. There are simply too many readers who just want to enjoy holding a book and reading it at leisure. (35)_____. Meanwhile, other readers can enjoy their savvy way of reading as well.

ANSWERS to choose from :

A. Several cases of piracy with novels have occurred.

B. In the coming years, e-books have no chances to succeed.

C. It saves the trouble of going to the library and carrying heavy books home.

D. The paper book readers are the loyal customers of these publishing companies.

E. For the health of precious eyesight, many consumers are not keen on eBooks.

F. Environmental awareness is a deciding buying factor for many consumers.

史上最強
GEPT Pro
企業英檢一本就夠
Mastering the GEPT Pro
The General English Proficiency Test Professional

Chapter. 05

第二回模擬試題
中文翻譯與解答

Mastering the GEPT Pro

he General English Proficiency Test

Professional

聽力測驗答案

1.	B	11.	B	21.	F	31.	D
2.	D	12.	D	22.	G	32.	C
3.	A	13.	D	23.	E	33.	A
4.	A	14.	C	24.	B	34.	B
5.	D	15.	C	25.	A	35.	B
6.	C	16.	B	26.	D		
7.	A	17.	C	27.	B		
8.	C	18.	C	28.	C		
9.	D	19.	B	29.	A		
10.	C	20.	C	30.	D		

閱讀測驗答案

1.	C	11.	C	21.	C	31.	C
2.	C	12.	C	22.	B	32.	F
3.	A	13.	B	23.	E	33.	E
4.	C	14.	C	24.	A	34.	A
5.	D	15.	A	25.	C	35.	D
6.	B	16.	B	26.	D		
7.	B	17.	B	27.	E		
8.	C	18.	F	28.	D		
9.	D	19.	E	29.	A		
10.	B	20.	A	30.	B		

第二回測驗

聽力測驗
第一部份：簡短對話與談話

本部分包括五篇簡短對話與四篇簡短談話，每篇對話與談話只播出一遍。每篇對話與談話後有一至三個相關的題目。請聽光碟放音機播出問題後，從試題冊上四個選項中選出最適合的答案。

1.

女：我聽說你這周末要再飛往香港。

男：對，我想要和我的客戶談一些細節。

女：你知道可以上網開視訊會議嗎？

男：我知道妳的意思，但是對我來說不是很好用。

女：要是你願意付交通費，我沒有意見。

問題：這位女士建議男子做什麼？

A. 飛往香港。

B. 與客戶開視訊會議。

C. 到其他地方旅行。

D. 學習新的電腦技能。

答案：B

2.

男：妳知道這次玩具展的所有產品都打六折嗎？

女：日本製玩具也包括在內嗎？

男：當然。事實上，我剛看到一些打五折的日本製玩具。

女：真划算！你可以帶我到那一區去嗎？

男：我這就帶妳去。

問題：這兩個人討論的主題是？

A. 日本製玩具的品質。

B. 玩具的來源地點。

C. 日本製玩具的安全。

D. 玩具展的優惠活動。

答案：D

3.

女：約翰，你知道如何使用投影片嗎？

男：這個嘛，我從未學過怎麼使用投影片。

女：怎麼會這樣？

男：我想可能是因為到現在我都沒機會做簡報。

女：既然如此，這個星期五就讓你第一次使用投影片吧。

問題：為什麼約翰從未學過怎麼使用投影片？
A. 他至今沒有機會學。
B. 他寧可讓其他人為他播放投影片。
C. 他不太會操作電腦軟體。
D. 他不喜歡做簡報。

答案：A

4.

男：妳知道為什麼羅柏特和湯姆合不來？
女：你難道沒聽說他們在爭奪經理職位？
男：看來這場競爭很激烈。
女：你大概是辦公室裡最後一個注意到這件事的人。
男：我當然不想要被捲進這場激烈競賽中。

問題：羅柏特和湯姆為什麼合不來？
A. 他們在爭奪經理職位。
B. 他們對同一位女同事感興趣。
C. 他們不喜歡彼此的個性。
D. 他們對很多工作程序的意見不合。

答案：A

5.

男：就妳的經驗看來，這工作對妳真是大材小用。

女：我喜歡這份工作的原因是因為我能夠在家作業，對我而言幾乎就像是兼差。

男：為什麼妳不想要在辦公室工作？

女：我有兩個年幼小孩要照顧，因此大部分辦公室的全職工作不適合我。

男：那麼妳何不先傳幾張草圖來給我？

問題：為什麼這位男士認為這工作對這位女士是大材小用？

A. 她的態度誠懇。

B. 她的圖像作品很優秀。

C. 她有很富創意的點子。

D. 她很有工作經驗。

答案：D

6.

男：很多人會在買相機的時候問該買什麼型式的好。就拿數位相機來說，各式各樣的機型、大小、功能、價錢都有。如果想要作明智的選購，必須先了解自己的真正需求和預算。還有一件該要注意的事情是，像是數位相機這樣的產品，科技進步飛快，五年前所買的數位相機今天可能會被當作古董。為了幫助您的選購過程，我們於每月第一天提供您資訊齊全的型錄。

問題6：這位男士正試圖做什麼？
A. 他在討論相機的製造過程。
B. 他在解釋數位相機的歷史。
C. 他在宣傳公司的相機。
D. 他在分析相機的組成。

答案：C

問題7：這位男士於結尾時作了什麼建議？
A. 購買相機的消費者看看他們每月的型錄。
B. 人們應該使用數位相機，而不用傳統相機。
C. 最新的相機總有最好的功能。
D. 大家應該買適合各種用途的數位相機。

答案：A

7.

女：我是您台北澳盛銀行的理財專員。前天您索取個人貸款的表格，但是那時我們沒有所需表格，現在我可以將您所需的表格於您方便時送去給您。這貸款計劃有效期限只到2013年9月30日。請您儘早回我電話，我的電話是(02) 2675-8942 轉 62，謝謝。

問題8：為什麼這位女士在電話留言機留話？

A. 為個人貸款作廣告。

B. 核對信用卡帳單。

C. 為了送貸款的申請表格。

D. 為了報告貸款利息。

答案：C

問題9：這位客戶想要申請什麼樣的貸款？

A. 成家貸款。

B. 汽車貸款。

C. 小型企業貸款。

D. 個人貸款。

答案：D

8.

男：自從我們的會員卡制度上路以來，我們預期到六月底的整體銷售量會至少增加7%，實際上從一月至六月的表現不如我們所預期的好：只有增加4%。我們希望到今年十二月底，我們能夠真正從會員卡獲利，銷售量會增加為前半年我們所見的兩倍。

問題10：這段簡短談話的主旨是什麼？

A. 會員卡與巨大銷售量。

B. 申請會員卡的資格。

C. 會員卡與銷售量的成長。

D. 會員卡的好處。

答案：C

問題11：說話者希望會員卡制度能帶來什麼？

A. 會員卡卡主能夠得到紅利。

B. 隨著時間延長，這制度能獲利更多。

C. 會員卡不能於其他家分店使用。

D. 說話者認為這個會員卡制度沒有用。

答案：B

問題12：說話者期待到今年年底的銷售增加量為何？

A. 7%

B. 14%

C. 4%

D. 8%

答案：D

9.

男：我是教師工會的代表張大成，我想要感謝因為看到我在臉書上宣布和平示威活動而來的人。我們來到這裡是為了爭取私立學校教師的基本權利，也就是退休金。這次罷工一度由6月30日延到7月31日，最後延到8月31日，我只能說我們已經給了有關當局充分回應我們訴求的機會。不幸的是，我們白等了。現在我們在8月31日這天於自由廣場和平靜坐，也就是很多學校新學年度的開始。雖然我們非常不願意見到這個狀況發生，但是如果這嚴重的議題仍然沒有獲得答案，接下來的幾天我們只能考慮罷教。

問題13：這位演說者是如何發動其他教師來參加這次罷工的？
A. 工會通訊。
B. 教師工會。
C. 勞工局。
D. 社群網站。

答案：D

問題14：這次的和平示威活動在哪一天舉行？
A. 6月30日。
B. 7月31日。
C. 8月31日。
D. 9月30日。

答案：C

問題15：這些老師們的訴求是？

A. 自由。

B. 更多的薪水。

C. 退休金。

D. 工作量減少。

答案：C

第二部份： 談話

本部份共 10 題。題目播放前將各有 30 秒的時間瀏覽圖表及新聞標題。每題播出一遍。

第 16 到 20 題為關於圖表上顯示台灣主要外銷國家所占百分比的問題；每題請聽光碟放音機播出的問題並參考圖表後，選出正確答案。

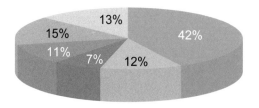

■ 中國&香港	42%
■ 美國	12%
■ 日本	7%
■ 歐洲	11%
■ 東盟國家	15%
■ 其他國家	13%

16. 這張圖表告訴我們關於台灣主要外銷國家的什麼資訊？

A. 每個主要外銷貿易的發展。

B. 每個主要外銷國家佔全部外銷國家的比率。

C. 每個主要外銷國家的未來潛力。

D. 每個主要外銷國家的經濟。

答案：B

17. 哪一個主要外銷國家於台灣外銷貿易佔有領先地位？

A. 日本。

B. 美國。

C. 中國和香港。

D. 歐洲。

答案：C

18. 根據這圖表，哪一個東北亞國家是台灣繼中國後的最大外銷國家？

A. 馬來西亞。

B. 新加坡。

C. 日本。

D. 印尼。

答案：C

19. 哪一個國家與台灣的外銷貿易和歐洲所佔比率相近？

A. 中國。

B. 美國。

C. 日本。

D. 香港。

答案：B

20. 這圖表上其他沒有列出來的國家佔多少比率？

A. 11%

B. 12%

C. 13%

D. 14%

答案：C

第 21 到 25 題為五篇新聞報導；每題請聽光碟放音機播出的新聞報導後, 從試題冊上 7 個選項中選出對應的標題。

21. 王國英語學校毫無預警歇業。上星期五傍晚，大部分孩子一如往常去上課，結果卻發現學校已經關門大吉。家長現在非常沮喪，因為他們所付的學費可能永遠無法退還。像這樣的英語學校都是私立的，經常不受政府法規約束。目前我們無法聯絡上王國英語學校

的負責人。

答案：F

22. 很多上班族為什麼在工作場所說謊的理由是，其他員工先說謊。大部分員工不再信任與他們共事的人和主管。為了要顧及他們自身的利益，他們決定像其他團員一樣，採用說謊策略。長遠來說，謊言破壞信賴的基礎。如果溝通沒有辦法去除謊言，那就不算是有建設性的溝通。在工作場所說謊的人應該要想想他們說謊的最終後果。

答案：G

23. 牙齒保險於西方不久前才開始，但是在台灣很少人有這樣的保險。牙齒保險背後的道理清楚且簡單：牙醫手術服務高昂的費用和其他疾病的治療相似，因此風險亦能以同樣方式管理。台灣消費者是否會跟上這個潮流，現在還有待觀察。然而大部分的牙醫師希望他們的病人有妥善的保險，這樣他們才能提供病人所負擔得起的必要醫療服務。

答案：E

24. 最近到過花蓮的人可能已經注意到日益增多的民宿，大部分是由夫妻檔所經營，有些在地主人有原住民背景。他們的室內設計和烹飪餐點表現出在地風味的特色。很快地，這些維護得很好的民宿吸引了不斷回來光顧的忠實顧客。雖然有些當地人對於觀光客於當地所造成的影響感到憂心，但是大部分人很高興看到經濟因此振興。

答案：B

25. 網路購物現今司空見慣，但是你聽過網路採買生活用品嗎？某人定時為你到超級市場採購生活用品，然後將採買到的東西送到你家大門口。很多網路購物公司現在正衡量提供這樣的服務的可能性。他們的主要問題是如何吸引足夠的消費者，讓他們願意為了這樣送貨到家的服務，簽定一年的合約。美國和歐洲的白領階級反應較熱烈，但是在台灣，大部分人似乎比較喜歡自己採買生活用品。

答案：A

A. 網路採買生活用品服務
B. 花蓮的民宿非常受歡迎
C. 海外學生保險
D. 公司員工的團購
E. 牙齒保險在台灣剛開始
F. 王國英語學校上星期五突然歇業
G. 工作場所的謊言

第三部份： 長篇對話與談話

本部份包括一段長篇談話與一段對話，每段談話或對話播出一遍。每段談話或對話前有45秒的時間閱讀五個問題，聽完談話或對話後，會有一分鐘的答題時間，每題請從 A、B、C、D 四個選項中選出正確答案。

女：今天我想要和你們談談廣告業界重要的法律問題。你們可能在最近的報紙上看到，好幾家的工業設計公司捲入版權法律糾紛。如果設計師對智慧財產權多加注意的話，這樣的案例是可以避免的，這一點在我們廣告公司來說也適用。每當你在想某個廣告台詞或是廣告中的某個場景，問一問你自己或你的團員：這些廣告台詞是原創的嗎？在別的廣告裡曾經出現過嗎？或是更直接問：我曾經在別地方看過這個嗎？我是否在潛意識裡從別人那裡抄襲到這個有創意的點子？要是真的如此，先確認你是否詢問過原作者或原設計師，你是否可以修改他們的點子，然後才加以使用。這麼做不只是有禮貌的行為，實際上能夠讓你避免捲入剽竊的法律糾紛。還有人認為可以剽竊國外他人的點子，直接在台灣使用。現今資訊於網路世界和其他媒體傳播快速，這樣的錯誤行為經常馬上就被發現。巨額資金會因此損失於賠償上，但是對一家台灣公司最壞的結果是，聲譽會被破壞到無法彌補的地步，特別是在國際上來說。

26. 這段談話的主旨是什麼？

A. 創意的思考和設計。

B. 分享點子和思想。

C. 創意和工業設計。

D. 版權和廣告。

答案：D

27. 這位演說者和聽者是從事哪一行業？

A. 圖像設計。

B. 廣告。

C. 出版業。

D. 行銷。

答案：B

28. 「剽竊」這個字可能於此內容中代表什麼意思？

A. 侵入民宅或非法使用。

B. 不實廣告或詐欺。

C. 未經允許使用或模仿。

D. 合作或人才流失。

答案：C

29. 這位演說者提到哪一個常見的錯誤？

A. 未經允許使用外國公司的點子。

B. 分析國外成功案例，運用他們的經驗。

C. 雇用外國的設計師，而不雇用台灣人才。

D. 將他們產品帶到國外，再也不回來。

答案：A

30. 這位演說者認為一家公司被抓到剽竊，什麼比罰錢還會更加受損？

A. 廣告的品質。

B. 公司的交易。

C. 廣告的客戶。

D. 公司的形象。

答案：D

男：歡迎您於台北國際筆記型電腦展最後一天來到金鳳凰公司。有什麼需要我為您服務的？

女：你可不可以為我介紹一些你們公司新型的筆記型電腦？

男：當然可以。我可以先問一下您的預算嗎？

女：事實上我對筆記型電腦的合理價格沒有概念，但是我室友有一台售價19,990的筆記型電腦。你們有那個價格內的筆記型電腦嗎？

男：當然有，請看看這台大螢幕的和那台非常輕的機型，這兩台都是 18,000 元。

女：可以打折給我嗎？目前我在師大學中文，而且我有帶我的美國護照。

男：我們可以給您學生九五折的優惠，只要您出示國際學生證。

女：這樣的話，我要買左邊那台粉紅色外殼的筆記型電腦。

男：我們明白很多學生都有金錢上的限制，所以我們提供筆記型電腦分期付款方案。甲方案分六個月付款，每個月 3000 元；乙方案分十二個月付款，每個月 1500 元，完全不需要付利息。

女：我想要乙方案。我可以用 VISA 信用卡付費嗎？

男：當然可以。不要忘了付款時向收銀員出示您的國際學生證。

女：我可以今天就把我的筆記型電腦帶回家還是要等人將筆記型電腦送到我住的地方？

男：您可以在乙方案合約和信用卡付費合約簽完名後，馬上帶走全新的筆記型電腦。

31. 這段對話發生於什麼地方？
A. 學生的合作商店。
B. 電腦硬體商店。
C. 電腦科學會議。
D. 國際筆記型電腦展。

答案：D

32. 這女子要出示什麼才能獲得折扣優惠？
A. 有效的護照。

B. 會員卡。

C. 國際學生證。

D. 駕照。

答案：C

33. 這女子每個月將必須要為新的筆記型電腦付多少錢？

A. 1500元。

B. 3000元。

C. 6000元。

D. 7500元。

答案：A

34. 這女子要如何付費購買筆記型電腦？

A. 用現金。

B. 用信用卡。

C. 一部分用現金，一部分用信用卡。

D. 用金融卡。

答案：B

35. 這女子在把新的筆記型電腦帶回家前，必須要先做什麼？

A. 付清第一期分期付款的金額。

B. 簽合約。

C. 付訂金。

D. 議價。

答案：B

閱讀能力測驗

第一部份：圖表、書信、短文

本部份包括圖表及數篇短文。每個圖表及每篇短文後有二至四個相關問題，每題後有四個選項，請根據圖表及短文提供的線索，由試題冊上 A、B、C、D 四個選項中選出最適合者為答案。請在答案紙上找到對應題號塗黑作答。

(1)
答案：1.（C）　　2.（C）　　3.（A）　　4.（C）

本文翻譯：

工作面試流程

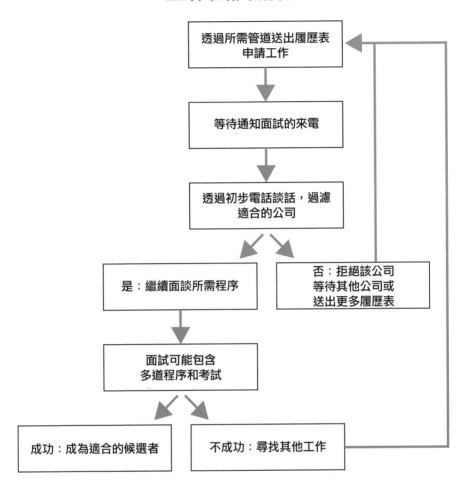

《字彙與片語》

　　　corporate culture　企業文化

　　　recommend　推薦

　　　supervise　督導

　　　guarantee　保證

1. 這張流程圖是做什麼用的？
A. 用來做公司行號的商業調查。
B. 用來取得人力資源的資訊。
C. 用來說明如何找工作。
D. 用來多了解企業文化。

2. 作者建議在最初電話通話裡要做什麼？
A. 表現自己優良的形象。
B. 認識人力資源主管。
C. 想辦法得到更多關於公司的資訊。
D. 讓他們對你的背景資料留下深刻的印象。

3. 誰會最覺得這張流程圖有用？
A. 正在找工作的人。
B. 經營小型企業者。
C. 想要對公司抱怨的顧客。
D. 督導一個部門的經理。

4. 下列關於這張流程圖的敘述何者不是真的？
A. 這張流程圖說明了找工作的好步驟。
B. 這張流程圖讓我們明白面試可能不只一次。
C. 這張流程圖絕對可以解決一個人的失業問題。
D. 這張流程圖主要是為了求職者所設計。

(2)

答案：5.(D)　　6.(B)　　7.(B)

本文翻譯：

寄件者：琳達‧陳
收件者：茱蒂‧瑞查森
主旨：手錶修理
日期：2013年6月29日星期六　上午10：09：54

親愛的瑞查森女士：

　　現在我想要談論的是關於我在2013年4月15日所買的手錶，保固期一年。這只手錶在我購買一個月後停了，然後，我到我原先買錶的零售錶店，有人告訴我電池已經沒電了。店員換了電池，但是一兩天前，那只換了新電池的手錶又停了。為了解決內部技術性問題，接著我到錶店去請店員幫忙。他請我填修理單，然後告訴我，他會將錶送到你們公司的技術支援部門。讓我大吃一驚的是，一星期後那家錶店的店員換成了一個新的女店員，而她找不到我的單子或資料。新的女店員幫不上我什麼忙，於是我只有寫信請負責亞洲總公司客戶服務的您幫忙。

　　請見附件裡一年保固書的掃描圖。

順頌　時綏

————————————

琳達・陳

電話：2479-8931

電子郵件：lindachen@yahoo.com.tw

————————————

《字彙與片語》

warranty period　保固期

customer service　客戶服務

attachment　附件

scanned picture　掃描圖

5. 琳達・陳女士為什麼寫這封電子郵件？

A. 抱怨她的手錶的價格。

B. 為了訂製自己專屬的手錶。

C. 為了感謝錶店的服務。

D. 詢問關於她的手錶修理的事項。

6. 第一次時那個店員如何修理琳達的手錶？

A. 他仔細檢查了那只錶。

B. 他換了手錶的電池。

C. 他請別人幫忙修錶。

D. 他給了琳達一只全新的手錶。

7. 茱蒂・瑞查森女士可能為何人？

A. 手錶零售商店的店員。

B. 客戶服務的主管。

C. 手錶設計師。

D. 手錶修理技師。

（3）

答案：8. (C)　　9. (D)　　10. (B)　　11. (C)

本文翻譯：

公司健康套裝方案

我們傑出的活力健身中心提供特別設計的健康套裝方案給公司行號，包括：

1. 健康檢查

223

2. 健康座談會

3. 減重計劃

4. 客製運動課程和計劃

5. 辦公室的專業訓練師

6. 結束時的專業評估

我們有信心，以上提到的服務可以幫助您的員工成功管理健康。健康檢查之後，我們會提供適合您員工需求之特別設計的訓練計劃和專業教練。我們的教練能鼓勵、追蹤、幫助您的員工達到開始時設下的目標。請聯絡張先生關於早鳥價的事項。

《字彙與片語》

　　　health check-up　健康檢查

　　　customized　客製化的

　　　evaluation　評估

　　　monitor　追蹤

8. 這短文的目的為何？

A. 宣傳夏日減重營。

B. 宣傳運動的重要性。

C. 為了吸引顧客來買運動套裝方案。

D. 為了宣布某家新健身中心的開幕。

9. 這個套裝方案不包含下列何者？
A. 運動教練。
B. 訓練時段。
C. 體重管理。
D. 客戶服務講座。

10. 在這裡「客製化的」最可能是什麼意思？
A. 根據傳統習俗的。
B. 特別為顧客設計的。
C. 與紀念品相關的。
D. 某種訓練機構。

11. 這廣告最可能是針對什麼人？
A. 餐廳的見習生。
B. 公司的實習生。
C. 小型企業負責人。
D. 公司的會計。

(4)

答案：12. (C)　　13. (B)　　14. (C)

本文翻譯：

台北，2013年8月21日

中國之旅的旅行日程

我們從2013年9月2日星期一到9月7日星期六的中國廣州團體商務旅行日程決定如下。如果有任何人有任何意見，請馬上寫電子郵件給我們的秘書黃小姐，她會再傳給我。班機與旅館住宿都已經預訂好了，但是如果有必要的話，我們至多可以延長兩天。

第一天　中午到達廣州的星辰酒店　與目標公司主管共進晚餐
第二天　參觀電腦晶片製造工廠
第三天　與供應廠商開會討論並簽合約
第四天　拜訪筆記型電腦零售商店
第五天　觀光
第六天　退房及搭機返台

如果沒有任何意見，我便會當作大家都接受這個旅行日程。謝謝大家。

總經理
傑克・潘

《字彙與片語》

       accommodation　住宿

       book　預訂

       maximum　至多

       contract　合約

12. 這是一張什麼時刻表？

A. 辦公室例行公事的時間表。

B. 待辦事項的時間表。

C. 商務旅行日程。

D. 在中國觀光的行程。

13. 他們最遲何時由廣州返抵台北？

A. 2013年9月7日。

B. 2013年9月9日。

C. 2013年9月2日。

D. 文中沒有提及。

14. 關於寫這個公告的人，何者不是真的？

A. 他是總經理。

B. 他在宣布一個商務旅行日程。

C. 他是這次唯一會去出差的人。

D. 他想要聽取其他人的意見。

(5)

答案：15.（A）　　16.（B）　　17.（B）

本文翻譯：

2012年訂單的來源地

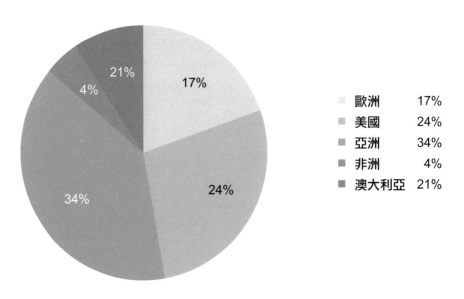

歐洲	17%
美國	24%
亞洲	34%
非洲	4%
澳大利亞	21%

《字彙與片語》

　　　order　訂單

　　　proportion　比例

destination　目的地

preference　偏好

15.　這張圓餅圖説明了什麼？

A.　訂單的來源地所佔比例。

B.　所製成的產品所佔百分比。

C.　商務旅行的目的地。

D.　產品偏好。

16.　根據這張圓餅圖，最多的訂單來自何處？

A.　澳大利亞。

B.　亞洲。

C.　歐洲。

D.　美國。

17.　這張圓餅圖最可能用於什麼地方？

A.　音樂廳。

B.　商務會議室。

C.　火車站。

D.　國際機場。

第二部份：長篇文章

（一）本部份包括兩篇文章，每篇文章分成五個段落。請從方框內的六個句子中，選出最符合每個段落大意的句子。

（1）

答案：18.（F）　19.（E）　20.（A）　21.（C）　22.（B）

本文翻譯：

A. 有機食品店的所有產品中只有非常少部分是真的有機食品。

B. 大家一般認為台灣有機食品的顧客會增加。

C. 為什麼價格這麼高？

D. 有機食品店在台灣的歷史比在美國還要長久。

E. 普遍說來，這裡共有四類有機食品店。

F. 在台灣的有機食品店形象很好。

在台灣的有機食品店

18.　現今在台灣有越來越多人在有機食品店購物。有機食品店通常都宣稱所有產品都是直接從農場送到市場的。有些提供剛從烤箱出爐的麵包和剛搾好的新鮮果汁供顧客品嚐，有些甚至提供烹飪課和

關於健康議題的座談會。

19. 如果我們分析這些又稱為健康食品店的有機食品店，我們會發現按照不同的創辦人共分為四類：提倡有機生活方式的醫生、宗教領導人物、從重大疾病康復者、環保人士。他們都相信飲食的重要性。

20. 即使他們的意圖都很良善，他們產品並非全都是真的有機食品；事實上，在這樣的商店內，平均只有20至30%的全部銷售產品可以被稱作完全「有機」。這樣似乎有欺騙嫌疑，但是實情是，在台灣大部分有機食品店必須要賣其他產品才能生存下來。

21. 消費者可能會問：為什麼有機食品這麼貴？一般來說，有機食品比非有機食品來得貴，尤其是在台灣。專家認為那是因為台灣的有機食品產業比其他國家起步晚得多，因此生產科技和行銷管道相較於大部分西方國家較不成熟。

22. 很多消費者認同有機食品的益處，但是因為價格高昂，他們雖然很想卻無法經常到有機食品店購物。隨著生產科技和行銷的進步，有機食品的價格可望為台灣消費者越來越接受。

《字彙與片語》

    environmentalist　環保人士

promote　提倡

intention　意圖

marketing channel　行銷管道

advantage　好處

acceptable　可接受的

(2)

答案：23. (E)　　24. (A)　　25. (C)　　26. (D)

本文翻譯：

A. 自雇風險雖高，但帶來更高的收入。

B. 很多自雇人士最後失業了。

C. 很多自雇者抱怨寂寞。

D. 是否成為自雇者要看工作性質而定。

E. 並非所有人都能成為良好自雇者和企業家。

你適合成為自雇者嗎？

23. 很多人聽到自雇，會聯想到企業家精神。能夠經營個人企業和自己當老闆，吸引了很多剛進入就業市場的人，尤其是年輕一輩的人。在決定為自己工作前，應該要仔細想想自己的人格特質，並非

所有人都能把危機處理得很好；還有一個必備條件是能管理與訓練
自己，能在與人隔絕的環境裡鞭策自己。

24. 剛開始時自雇者的平均所得比傳統受雇者來得低，但是隨著時
間延長，他們的所得超過傳統受雇者的平均所得。整體來說，自雇
者所賺的錢的確較傳統受雇者來得多。自雇者工作內容自然而然和
作決策和管理風險有關。管理個人小型企業則需要企業家精神。

25. 能夠在自己的空間，以自己速度工作的自由，聽起來如此吸引
人，但是與社會缺乏接觸常帶來寂寞感。與其他人隔絕可以不受煩
人同事的干擾，但是長久下來缺乏社會互動，對人很不健康。為了
解決這個問題，有些人和其他人合租辦公室空間。

26. 除此之外，將個人工作性質考慮進去才算明智。作家、翻譯
者、自由寫手適合當自雇者；另一方面而言，如果一個人的工作必
須要經常和團員腦力激盪，自雇可能就不是很聰明的作法了。

《字彙與片語》

　　entrepreneurship　企業家精神

　　particularly　尤其

　　personal characteristic　人格特質

　　surpass　超過

　　in the long run　長久下來

brainstorm　腦力激盪

（二）本部份包括兩篇文章，每篇文章各有四個及六個空格，請由文章下方方框內提供的選項中，選出正確的句子放回文章空格。每篇文章各標示一句例答供參考。選項中有一個句子不會用到。

(1)

答案：27.(E)　　28.(D)　　29.(A)　　30.(B)

本文翻譯：

領導力

在一個像公司行號的組織內，從執行長到小部門主管的經理角色都需要有能力來帶領團隊，通稱為「領導力」。關於領導力的工作坊和書籍的需求量很大，而幾乎每天都有新理論和新作法出現。整體而言，良好的領導技巧有四個必要的特質。

力量：(27)_____.　當然，除了社交技巧外，對於公司和所從事產業的了解必須透徹。

温暖：溫暖通常伴隨同理心和親切感而存在，有時還有非凡的領導魅力。(28)_____. 在很多台灣公司裡，雇主經常被視作父母親的角色。有些人甚至用「權謀政治家」來描述這些讓人同時又怕又愛的領導人物。

按優先順序處理事情：所有領導人物都必須要非常能夠按優先順序處理任務與議題，並依照事情的輕重緩急來安排時間和金錢這樣的寶貴資源。在當前不穩定的經濟狀況，需要明智的領導者來決定何時採取行動，何時設停損點。(29)_____.

團結：(30)_____. 每個成員都應該明瞭自己對目標該做的貢獻。一個領導應該深知團隊成員的忠誠度，有效處理會危害團隊團結的人物。

力量、溫暖、按優先順序處理事情、團結是商業界傑出領導者的特徵。這些特徵看起來簡單，一個新手領導者卻可能會覺得不易駕馭。

《字彙與片語》
  charisma　非凡的領導魅力
  Machiavellian　權謀政治家
  the stop loss point　停損點

novice　新手

可選擇的選項：

A. 有效按優先順序處理事情是使團隊發揮最大功能的必備技巧。

B. 為了要確保團隊完全團結，必須要建立清楚的共同目標。

C. 對工作結果優秀的員工非常應該要獎勵。

D. 良好的人格特質通常是一家公司優秀主管的特徵。

E. 一家公司能力強的領導者首先要擁有領導團隊的力量。

(2)

答案：31.(C)　　32.(F)　　33.(E)　　34.(A)　　35.(D)

本文翻譯：

電子書的優缺點

就如同科技進步對其他領域的衝擊一樣，電子書對現在我們的閱讀方式影響深遠。很多讀者從未預期到這樣的現代閱讀方式，仍然正

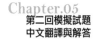

在觀望市場。有的人，特別是年輕人，正擁抱並享受著電子書的好處。

這裡有些主要好處是電子書的讀者會毫不猶豫地告訴朋友的：

首先，相較於傳統的紙本書籍，電子書讓運送讀物輕鬆許多。所有讀者只要購買一個通常可上網或有其他相關服務的電子配備。(31)_____.

其次，電子書不使用紙張，有助於環境保護。(32)_____. 知道沒有任何一棵樹因為產品而犧牲，讓讀者的良心安穩。

最後而非最不重要的一點是電子書包含多媒體和容易搜尋、標示重點、儲存，甚至編輯的電子文字。年長的讀者可以因為老花眼而輕鬆地放大字體。和別人分享電子檔案比起從前來得容易多了。

關於視力的議題同時也可能是缺點。很多人因為過長時間使用電腦而造成了視力問題。現在市面上的閱讀機比起一般筆記型電腦螢幕甚至還要小。(33)_____.

對出版業來說，盜版是電子書的本質自然會引起的災難。(34)_____. 很多出版社因此到現在還不願意發行電子書。

許多的出版社對於傳統紙本書信心滿滿，實在有太多的讀者就是想要享受捧者一本書慢慢閱讀的樂趣。(35)_____. 而其他讀者同時也可以享受新潮的閱讀方式。

《字彙與片語》

       anticipate　預期

       hesitation　猶豫

       device　設備；裝置

       multi-media　多媒體

       piracy　盜版

       savvy　聰明的；資訊豐富的

可選擇的選項：

A. 過去發生過許多小說的盜版案例。

B. 在未來幾年中，電子書沒有成功機會。

C. 省下上圖書館和背書回家的麻煩。

D. 紙本書讀者是這些出版社的忠實顧客。

E. 因為寶貴的視力健康，很多消費者對電子書興趣缺缺。

F. 環保意識是很多消費者購買的決定因素。

MP3

Chapter. 06

必背420字

Mastering the GEPT Pro
The General English Proficiency Test
Professional

史上最強
GEPT Pro
企業英檢一本就夠

如何準備字彙？

商業英文的字彙包羅萬象，平日就要養成好習慣，多閱讀英文報章雜誌和財經新聞報導，不斷充實相關字彙。

沒有人能夠於短時間背到所有會出現於考題的單字，因此，無論在聽或讀英文時，能夠依照上下文猜測、推論陌生單字字義的能力，尤其是不熟的關鍵字，在考場上就顯得特別重要，而這樣的能力必須靠自己不斷隨時自我訓練，通常並非一蹴可幾。平時學習英文時，便要掌握這樣推測的原則儲備單字量，不建議一看到新單字，就馬上查字典，例如在聆聽英文時，往往可以依照情境內容，合理推測沒聽過的單字和片語的含義；而於閱讀時，如果遇到了新單字，可能無法一眼馬上就判斷出正確含義，但只要透過略讀，快速分析上下文，再配合基本字根、字首的知識，多半十之八九能靠推論得到極相近的字義。

因篇幅有限，以下所整理出的單字表，為最常見的英文商業相關字彙，不但對於準備《企業英檢》有極大的幫助，也可以用來大幅提昇個人於商場上的英文溝通能力；希望讀者研讀本書之後，除了能夠高分通過《企業英檢》，於實際生活中也能靈活運用本書各章內容，讓英語變為職場利器，這樣也就達到本書的最終目的了。

A

ability　　n.　能力；能耐

【同義詞】power, skill, talent, competence

abuse　　v.　濫用，妄用

【同義詞】misuse, maltreat, misapply, spoil, harm

acceptance　　n.　接受；領受

【同義詞】accepting, taking, receipt, reception

access　　n.　接近，進入；接近的機會，進入的權利

【同義詞】way of approach, entry

accomplish　　v.　完成，實現，達到

【同義詞】realize, do, complete, perform

achievement　　n.　達成; 完成

【同義詞】accomplishment, feat, deed, act

activity　　n.　活動; 活動力

【同義詞】energy, movement, action

actual　　n.　實際的, 事實上的

【同義詞】factual, authentic, genuine, real

advertisement　　n.　廣告, 宣傳

【同義詞】announcement, blurb, statement, broadcast

add　　v.　添加; 增加

【同義詞】unite, increase, total, join

administration　　n.　管理, 經營; 監督

【同義詞】rule, authority, governance, government

admit   v.　承認

【同義詞】consent, confess, acknowledge

adolescent   a.　青年的, 青春期的

【同義詞】young, youthful, juvenile, teenage

adopt   v.　採取; 採納; 吸收

【同義詞】assume, choose

advocate   v.　擁護; 提倡; 主張

【同義詞】defend, support

affect   v.　影響

【同義詞】influence, sway, move, touch

agency   n.　代辦處, 經銷處, 代理機構

【同義詞】operation, office, work, management

alternative　v.　兩者(或若干)中擇一的

【同義詞】choice, substitute, replacement

annual　a.　一年的；一年一次的

【同義詞】yearly, once a year, anniversary

apply　v.　應用；實施

【同義詞】employ, use, utilize, exercise

appreciate　v.　欣賞，賞識

【同義詞】value, cherish, treasure, prize

approach　v.　接近，研討

【同義詞】come near, advance, proximate, approximate

appropriate　a.　適當的, 恰當的, 相稱的

【同義詞】suitable, becoming, fitting, proper

argue　v.　爭論, 辯論；爭吵

【同義詞】reason, object, persuade

arrange　v.　整理；佈置

【同義詞】array, adjust, organize, classify

article　n.　物品；文章；條款

【同義詞】item, composition, treatise, report, essay

associate　v.　聯想, 把...聯想在一起

【同義詞】join, connect, unite, combine

assume　v.　以為；假定為

【同義詞】suppose, presume, suspect, believe

attachment　n.　連接；附件

【同義詞】connection

attempt　n.　試圖；企圖；試圖做

【同義詞】try, endeavor, undertake, strive

attention　　n.　注意; 注意力; 專心

【同義詞】care, courtesy, concern, consideration

attitude　　n.　態度, 意見, 看法

【同義詞】viewpoint, standpoint, position, opinion

attract　　v.　吸; 吸引

【同義詞】tempt, charm, allure, fascinate

auction　　v.　拍賣

【同義詞】public bidding

audience　　n.　聽眾, 觀眾; 讀者群

【同義詞】spectators, viewers, listeners, hearers

authority　　n.　權, 權力; 職權

【同義詞】jurisdiction, dominion, sovereignty

available　　a.　可用的，在手邊的；可利用的

【同義詞】handy, convenient, obtainable, ready

average　　a.　平均的

【同義詞】usual, common, ordinary, general

avoid　　v.　避開，躲開

【同義詞】shun, evade, escape, eschew

aware　　a.　知道的，察覺的

【同義詞】knowing, conscious, realizing

balance　　n.　平衡，結餘

【同義詞】equipoise, poise, stasis

banquet　n.　宴會，盛宴

【同義詞】affair, feast, formal dinner

bargain　n.　協議

【同義詞】agreement, contract, sale

barter　v.　以物易物

【同義詞】trade, deal, swap, exchange

basis　n.　基礎，根據；準則

benefit　n.　利益，好處；優勢

【同義詞】advantage, profit, gain, good

bid　v.　命令；出價，投標

【同義詞】command, charge, direct, instruct, order

bill　n.　帳單

【同義詞】invoice, statement, record, account

blame　n.　責備，指責

【同義詞】charge, accuse, impeach, indict

block　n.　封鎖，阻止，妨礙

【同義詞】clog, obstruct, hinder, check

blockbuster　n.　轟動一時的電影巨片

【同義詞】hit, megahit, success, winner

board　n.　委員會；理事會；董事會

【同義詞】association, chamber, council, society, committee

boost　v.　推動；促進

【同義詞】lift, increase, push, shove

bother　v.　煩擾，打攪

【同義詞】concern, annoy, trouble, fuss

bounce　　v.　彈起，彈回

【同義詞】eject, dismiss, expel, oust, out

boycott　　v.　聯合抵制；拒絕參加(或購買等)

【同義詞】strike, revolt, blackball, ban

budget　　n.　預算；預算費；生活費，經費

【同義詞】ration, allowance

bureau　　n.　事務處，聯絡處；(政府機構的)局、司、署、處

【同義詞】agency, branch, division, department, office

business　　n.　職業；日常工作

【同義詞】work, function, occupation, affair

campaign   n.   戰役

【同義詞 】drive, cause, movement, crusade

candidate   n.   候選人；候補者

【同義詞 】seeker, nominee, applicant

capital   a. n.   首位的；首都；首府

【同義詞 】important, leading, top, chief

capture   v.   捕獲；俘虜

【同義詞 】apprehend, seize, arrest, imprison

career   n.   (終身的)職業

【同義詞 】vocation, trade, calling, profession

case   n.   事實，實情，實例

【同義詞】sample, instance, condition, state

 celebrate　v.　慶祝

【同義詞】proclaim, observe, commemorate

charge　v.　索價；對...索費；課(稅)

【同義詞】ask, command, demand

check　v.　檢查，檢驗，核對

【同義詞】stop, control, restrain, curb

choice　n.　選擇，抉擇

【同義詞】selection, preference, pick, decision

claim　v.　(根據權利而提出的)要求

【同義詞】demand, require

client　n.　委託人，(律師等的)當事人

【同義詞】customer, prospect, patron

collapse　v.　倒塌

【同義詞】fail, crash, topple, break down

commerce　n.　商業, 貿易, 交易

【同義詞】trade, business, dealings

common　a.　普通的; 常見的

【同義詞】public, general, usual, familiar

community　n.　社區, 共同社會; 共同體

【同義詞】society, people, colony, district

competition　n.　競爭, 角逐

【同義詞】contest, game, match, tournament

complain　v.　抱怨, 發牢騷

【同義詞】grumble, squawk, find fault

complete　v.　完成，結束

【同義詞】finish, conclude, terminate, end

concept　n.　概念，觀念，思想

【同義詞】thought, notion, idea, opinion

concern　v.　關於

【同義詞】interest, affect, trouble, involve

conference　n.　（正式)會議；討論會，協商會

【同義詞】meeting, convention, council, caucus

confirm　v.　證實；確定

【同義詞】establish, verify, substantiate, prove

consider　v.　考慮，細想

【同義詞】think, study, ponder, reflect

consumer　　n.　消費者；消耗者

【同義詞】user, buyer, purchaser, shopper

context　　n.　上下文；文章脈絡

【同義詞】connection, contextual relation, following words, next sentences

contribution　　n.　貢獻

【同義詞】charity, donation, philanthropy

control　　v.　控制；支配；管理

【同義詞】command, influence, master, restrain

controversial　　a.　爭論的；可疑的

【同義詞】polemical, dialectic, factious, contradictory

convince　　v.　使確信，使信服；說服

【同義詞】persuade, assure, promise, guarantee

corporate　a.　法人(組織)的

【同義詞】commercial, marketable, mass-market

correspondence　n.　一致；符合

【同義詞】similarity, analogy, likeness, resemblance

cost　n.　費用；成本

【同義詞】price, charge, rate, amount

courier　n.　送遞急件(或外交信件)的信差

【同義詞】messenger, runner

credibility　n.　可信性；確實性

【同義詞】believability, likelihood, plausibility, validity

crisis　n.　危機；緊急關頭；轉折點

【同義詞】emergency, critical point, crucial period, turning point

critic　　n.　批評家, 評論家

【同義詞 】commentator, reviewer, expositor, expounder

current　　a.　現時的, 當前的; 現行的

【同義詞 】flow, stream, prevalent, present

damage　　v.　損害; 損失

【同義詞 】harm, hurt, impair, spoil

deadline　　n.　截止期限, 最後限期

【同義詞 】a date before which something must be done

deal　　n.　交易

【同義詞 】trade, traffic

debt n. 債，借款

【同義詞】obligation, amount due

decade n. 十，十年

【同義詞】a set of 10, a period of 10 years

deceive v. 欺騙，蒙蔽

【同義詞】beguile, trick, hoax, dupe

decent a. 正派的；合乎禮儀的

【同義詞】respectable, proper, correct, right

decline v. 下降，下跌；減少；衰退，衰落

【同義詞】refuse, reject, sink, fail

deduction n. 扣除，減除

【同義詞】abatement, discount, reduction

deficit　　n.　不足額；赤字

【同義詞】inadequacy, insufficiency, lack, shortage, undersupply, want

define　　v.　解釋，給...下定義

【同義詞】explain, describe, clarify, fix

deliver　　v.　投遞；傳送；運送

【同義詞】transfer, pass, consign, give

demand　　v.　要求，請求

【同義詞】ask, inquire, require

depression　　n.　沮喪，意氣消沈；不景氣，蕭條

【同義詞】sadness, inactivity, recession, slump

design　　v.　設計；構思：繪製

【同義詞】sketch, draw, paint, picture

desire　v.　渴望；要求

【同義詞 】wish, want, fancy, lust

desperate　a.　情急拼命的，鋌而走險的

【同義詞 】frantic, wild, reckless, rash

destabilize　v.　暗中顛覆(反對政權)；使不穩定

【同義詞 】make unstable

develop　v.　使成長；使發達；發展

【同義詞 】grow, flourish, mature, progress, evolve

dialog　n.　對話；交談

【同義詞 】conversation, talk, speech, words

director　n.　主管；署長；局長；處長；主任

【同義詞 】administrator, executive, bureaucrat, functionary

disagree　　v.　不一致, 不符

【同義詞】differ, quarrel, conflict, dispute

dismiss　　v.　讓...離開; 把...打發走

【同義詞】discharge, expel, send away

display　　v.　陳列; 展出

【同義詞】demonstrate, illustrate, exhibit, show

dispute　　v.　爭論; 爭執

【同義詞】argue, debate, quarrel, oppose

dividend　　n.　紅利; 股息

【同義詞】share, portion, quantum, surplus

division　　n.　分開, 分割

【同義詞】separation, segmentation, disconnection, dismemberment

document　n.　公文, 文件

【同義詞】writing, paper, certificate, credentials

domestic　a.　家庭的, 家事的; 國家的, 國內的

【同義詞】household, home, family, internal

dominance　n.　優勢; 支配(地位), 統治(地位)

【同義詞】ascendance, supremacy, domination, predominance, sovereignty

draw　v.　劃, 畫, 繪製, 描寫

【同義詞】pull, drag, haul, attract

drive　v.　駕車旅行; (開車)兜風; 車程

【同義詞】steer, ride, handle, operate

drop　v.　(聲音, 風等)變弱; (價格, 溫度等)下降

【同義詞】depress, lower, throw, throw down

drug　　n.　藥品, 藥材

【同義詞】cure, medicine, medicament, medication

earn　　v.　賺得, 掙得

【同義詞】get, gain, obtain, make

earnings　　n. 收入, 工資

【同義詞】wages, salary, gains, profit, return, revenue, yield

effective　　a.　有效的

【同義詞】effectual, efficacious, efficient, productive

efficiency　　n.　效率; 效能; 功效

【同義詞】effectiveness, effectualness, efficacy, productiveness

effort　n.　努力，盡力

【同義詞】attempt, try, endeavor, exertion

elect　v.　選舉；推選

【同義詞】choose, pick, select, appoint

eliminate　v.　排除，消除，消滅

【同義詞】remove, discard, reject, exclude

emerge　v.　浮現；出現

【同義詞】appear, come out, come into view, loom

employee　n.　受雇者，雇工，雇員，從業員工

【同義詞】worker, staffer, hired hand, hireling

encourage　v.　鼓勵；慫恿

【同義詞】support, urge, invite, promote

enter　　v.　進入

【同義詞】join, go into, penetrate, pierce

enthusiasm　　n.　熱心, 熱情, 熱忱

【同義詞】eagerness, earnestness, keenness, fervency

environment　　n.　環境; 四周狀況

【同義詞】atmosphere, climate, context, environs, setting, surroundings

equipment　　n.　配備, 裝備

【同義詞】apparatus, gear, hardware, materials, outfit

establish　　v.　建立; 設立; 創辦

【同義詞】fix, set, settle, build

eventually　　adv.　最後, 終於

【同義詞】finally, ultimately, in time

evidence　　n.　證據；證詞；證人；物證

【同義詞】facts, proof, grounds, data

excess　　n.　超越, 超過；超額量；過量, 過剩

【同義詞】oversupply, superabundance, superfluity, surplus

expand　　v.　展開, 張開(帆, 翅等)

【同義詞】amplify, develop, elaborate, enlarge

expect　　v.　預計...可能發生(或來到)；預料

【同義詞】anticipate, await, think, suppose

expert　　n.　專家；能手；熟練者

【同義詞】skillful, adept, apt, handy

explore　　v.　探測；探勘；在...探險

【同義詞】search, hunt, look, research

extent　n.　廣度, 寬度; 程度, 範圍

【同義詞】magnitude, measure, degree, quantity

facility　n.　能力, 技能; 設備; 場所

【同義詞】edifice, building, structure, plant

fair　a.　公正的; 公平的; 誠實的

【同義詞】just, equitable, impartial, unbiased, objective

favorite　a.　特別喜愛的

【同義詞】choice, cherished, prized, beloved

figure　n.　數字, 數量; 價格, 金額

【同義詞】digit, number, numeral, numeric

file　v.　歸檔

【同義詞】sort, classify, group, categorize

financial　a.　財政的；金融的；金融界的

【同義詞】fiscal, money, monetary

fine　v.　罰金，罰款

【同義詞】penalize, amerce

firm　n.　商號，商行，公司

【同義詞】company, business, enterprise, corporation

fix　v.　修理；校準；整理；收拾

【同義詞】mend, repair, adjust, regulate

focus　v.　調焦，聚焦

【同義詞】concentrate, adjust

folk　n.　（某一民族，種族或社會階層中的）廣大成員

【同義詞】people, persons, society, public

force　v.　強迫，迫使

【同義詞】compel, make, drive, oblige

form　v.　塑造，養成

【同義詞】develop, compose, make, create

former　a.　從前的，前者的，前任的

【同義詞】earlier, past, previous, preceding

found　v.　建立；建造

【同義詞】establish, start, create, originate

fragile　a.　易碎的；脆的；易損壞的

【同義詞】delicate, frail, slight, dainty

frank   a.   坦白的；直率的；真誠的

【同義詞】open, candid, sincere, straightforward

fraud   n.   欺騙(行為)；詭計；騙局

【同義詞】cheating, trickery, dishonesty, swindle

frequency   n.   頻繁，屢次；頻率

【同義詞】commonness, frequentness, prevalence

fuel   n.   燃料

【同義詞】combustible

fund   n.   資金，基金，專款

【同義詞】stock, supply, resources, assets

gain v. 得到；獲得，贏得（戰爭，訴訟等）

【同義詞】get, obtain, secure, acquire

generate v. 產生，發生（熱，電，光等）；造成，引起

【同義詞】produce, cause, create, originate

genuine a. 真的；非偽造的；名副其實的

【同義詞】real, true, authentic, pure

goods n. 商品；貨物

【同義詞】belongings, property, holdings, possessions

grant v. 同意，准予

【同義詞】give, donate, present, bestow

guarantee v. 保證；擔保

【同義詞】promise, secure, pledge, swear

guilty　　a.　有罪的，犯...罪的

【同義詞】criminal, blameworthy, culpable, to blame

gym　　n.　體育館，健身房

【同義詞】gymnasium, health club

handle　　v.　操作；處理

【同義詞】touch, feel, finger, manipulate

head　　v.　率領；出發

【同義詞】lead, precede, initiate, come first

headline　　n.　(報紙等的)標題；大標題

【同義詞】caption, title, heading, head

headquarters　　n.　（軍, 警的)司令部, 總部, 總署; 司

【同義詞 】base, central station, main office

hire　　v.　租借; 雇用

【同義詞 】employ, engage, use, lease

honor　　n.　榮譽; 名譽, 面子

【同義詞 】glory, fame, renown, respect

host　　n.　主人, 東道主

【同義詞 】receptionist, proprietor

illegal　　a.　不合法的, 非法的; 違反規則的

【同義詞 】unlawful, criminal, illegitimate

impact　v.　衝擊，撞擊；產生影響

【同義詞 】affect, impress, influence, move, reach, strike, sway

improve　v.　改進，改善；增進

【同義詞 】better, ameliorate, meliorate, perfect

incentive　n.　刺激；鼓勵；動機

【同義詞 】motive, stimulus, encouragement, inducement

increase　v.　增大；增加；增強

【同義詞 】enlarge, extend, expand, augment

indicate　v.　指示；指出

【同義詞 】show, exhibit, demonstrate, disclose

inspiration　n.　靈感；鼓舞人心的人事物

【同義詞 】stimulus, stimulation, arousal, incentive

install v. 任命, 使就職; 安裝, 設置

【同義詞】admit, establish, inaugurate, instate

instead adv. 作為替代

【同義詞】in place of, rather than, in lieu of

institute n. 學會, 學社, 協會

【同義詞】chamber, club, council, organization, association, society

interest n. 興趣; 關注; 愛好

【同義詞】concern, curiosity, share, portion

introduce v. 介紹, 引見

【同義詞】inaugurate, institute, launch, innovate

invest v. 投資

【同義詞】venture, stake, empower, place

involve　　v.　使捲入，連累；牽涉

【同義詞】include, concern, affect, entail

issue　　n.　問題，爭論，爭議

【同義詞】cause, principle, campaign, topic

item　　n.　項目；品目；條款；細目

【同義詞】part, segment, portion, subdivision

jail　　n.　監獄；拘留所

【同義詞】jailhouse, lockup, prison

jobless　　a.　失業的

【同義詞】unemployed

join   v.   連結；使結合

【同義詞】connect, fasten, clasp, unite

journal   n.   日報；雜誌；期刊

【同義詞】account, log, diary, chronicle

justify   v.   證明...是正當的；為...辯護

【同義詞】warrant, authorize, legitimate, legitimatize

juvenile   a.   少年的

【同義詞】young, youthful

Track 63

keen   a.   熱心的, 熱衷的, 深切的

【同義詞】delicate, fine, acute, perceptive, quick, sensitive, sharp

key　a.　重要的，基本的，關鍵的

【同義詞】important, fundamental, central, chief, dominant, leading, main

knock　v.　相撞，碰擊

【同義詞】hit, strike, punch, jab

label　n.　貼紙；標籤；商標

【同義詞】name, brand, title, tag

labor　n.　勞動

【同義詞】work, employment, job, occupation

lack　v.　缺少；沒有

【同義詞】want, need, require, fall short

lawyer　　n.　律師

【同義詞】attorney, attorney-at-law, counsel, counselor

legacy　　n.　遺產; 遺贈

【同義詞】bequest, birthright, heritage, inheritance

legal　　a.　法律上的, 有關法律的

【同義詞】lawful, legitimate, licit, authorized

legitimate　　a.　合法的

【同義詞】lawful, rightful, allowed, legal

license　　n.　許可, 特許

【同義詞】permission, allowance, consent, vouchsafement

lifestyle　　n.　生活方式

【同義詞】culture, life, civilization, society

line　n.　繩, 線, 索; 列, 排

【同義詞】column, cue, file, queue, range, string

link　v.　連接, 結合; 聯繫

【同義詞】unite, connect, join, combine

list　n.　表; 名冊; 目錄

【同義詞】enumeration, schedule, record, register

lobby　v.　進行遊説; 施加壓力

【同義詞】influence, sway

local　a.　地方性的; 當地的, 本地的

【同義詞】regional, limited, particular, restricted

locate　v.　確定...的地點(或範圍)

【同義詞】discover, find, uncover, unearth

lottery　　n.　獎券, 彩票; 摸彩, 抽籤

【同義詞】raffle, drawing

lower　　v.　放下, 降下; 減低; 貶低

【同義詞】drop, depress, plunge, immerse

loyalty　　n.　忠誠; 忠心

【同義詞】attachment, commitment, dedication, faith, devotion

luxury　　n.　奢侈, 奢華

【同義詞】luxuriousness, luxe, sumptuousness, lavishness

mainstream　　n.　主流

【同義詞】major trend

281

majority　n.　多數, 過半數, 大多數

【同義詞 】plurality, bulk, mass, the must

manufacture　v.　(大量)製造, 加工

【同義詞 】make, invent, create, fashion

mark　v.　做記號於, 標明

【同義詞 】label, tag, ticket

market　n.　市場; 股票市場; 市集

【同義詞 】store, shop, mart

massive　a.　大量的; 大規模的

【同義詞 】big, large, heavy, solid

material　n.　材料, 原料

【同義詞 】substance, fabric, stuff, matter

matter　　n.　事情；問題；事件

【同義詞】material, substance, composition, content

meanwhile　　adv.　其時，其間

【同義詞】at the same time

measure　　v.　測量；計量

【同義詞】size, grade, rank, compare

media　　n.　工具；媒體（medium的複數）

【同義詞】instruments, tools, agents, implements

medical　　a.　醫學的；醫術的；醫療的

【同義詞】healing, curative, therapeutic, therapeutical

merchandise　　n.　商品，貨物

【同義詞】goods, wares, commodities, products

merger　n.　（公司等的)合併

【同義詞 】combination, connection, union, unification

mission　n.　使命，任務；外交使團；佈道團

【同義詞 】errand, business, purpose, task

monitor　v.　監控，監聽，監測，監視

【同義詞 】cover, watch, keep an eye on

mortgage　n.　抵押

【同義詞 】pledge, guaranty, security, contract

motivate　v.　給...動機；刺激；激發

【同義詞 】urge, drive, move, propel

negative　　a.　否定的; 否認的

【同義詞】nullifying, voiding, canceling

negotiate　　v.　談判, 協商, 洽談

【同義詞】arrange, settle, mediate, intervene

network　　n.　網狀系統, 網路

【同義詞】organization, order, system, arrangement

notice　　v.　通知, 貼示

【同義詞】note, observe, heed, regard

object　　v.　反對

【同義詞】expostulate, kick, protest, remonstrate

obtain　v.　得到，獲得

【同義詞】get, acquire, gain, secure

obvious　a.　明顯的；顯著的

【同義詞】understandable, apparent, clear, plain

occasion　n.　場合，時刻；重大活動，盛典

【同義詞】time, instance, case, spot

odds　n.　機會，可能性；成功的可能性

【同義詞】probability, chance

offer　v.　給予，提供；拿出，出示

【同義詞】present, propose, try, submit

official　a.　官方的；公務上的

【同義詞】authorized, sanctioned

operate　v.　工作；運作；運轉

【同義詞】work, run, manage, conduct

opportunity　n.　機會；良機

【同義詞】chance, occasion, time, opening

opposition　n.　反對；反抗；對抗

【同義詞】defiance, resistance

order　n.　順序，次序

【同義詞】arrangement, condition, state, manner

organize　v.　組織；安排

【同義詞】arrange, classify, systematize, categorize

package　n.　包裹；包

【同義詞 】bundle, pack, packet, parcel

part　n.　一部分, 部分

【同義詞 】fragments, particles, chunks, portion

participate　v.　參加, 參與

【同義詞 】partake, take part in, have a hand in, enter into

particular　a.　特殊的；特定的；特別的

【同義詞 】special, unusual, different, meticulous

perception　n.　感知, 感覺；察覺

【同義詞 】understanding, comprehension, apprehension, grasp

permit　v.　允許, 許可, 准許

【同義詞 】allow, consent, let, grant

perspective　n.　透視圖；觀點，看法

【同義詞】view, vista, prospect, picture

pick　v.　挑選，選擇

【同義詞】choose, select, gather, cull

plant　v.　栽種，播種；設置

【同義詞】establish, fix, root, settle

plot　v.　陰謀；祕密計劃

【同義詞】plan, scheme, intrigue, maneuver

popularity　n.　普及，流行；大眾化

【同義詞】fashionableness, favor, hotness, modishness, vogue

population　n.　人口

【同義詞】inhabitants, people

portion n. （一）部分

【同義詞 】part, share, division, segment

position n. 位置，地點，方位

【同義詞 】place, location, situation, spot

positive a. 確定的；確實的

【同義詞 】sure, definite, certain, absolute

possess v. 擁有，持有；具有；佔有

【同義詞 】own, have, hold, control

possibility n. 可能性

【同義詞 】chance, potentiality, feasibility, practicability

potential a. 潛在的，可能的

【同義詞 】possible, promising, hidden, likely

practical　　a.　實踐的, 實際的

【同義詞】utilitarian, useful, pragmatic

price　　n.　價格, 價錢

【同義詞】cost, value, amount, rate

procedure　　n.　程序; 手續; 步驟

【同義詞】process, course, measure, custom

profit　　n.　利潤, 盈利; 收益, 紅利

【同義詞】gain, benefit, advantage, earnings

project　　n.　計劃; 企劃　　

【同義詞】arrangement, blueprint, program, plan, scheme, strategy, system

property　　n.　財產, 資產; 所有物

【同義詞】possession, holdings, belongings

proposal　n.　建議, 計劃

【同義詞 】plan, scheme, suggestion, offer

prosperity　n.　興旺, 繁榮, 昌盛, 成功

【同義詞 】wealth, riches, fortune, affluence

protect　v.　保護, 防護

【同義詞 】guard, defend, shield, screen

prove　v.　證明, 證實

【同義詞 】show, verify, check, confirm

provide　v.　提供

【同義詞 】supply, give, furnish

publisher　n.　出版(或發行)者; 出版(或發行)公司

【同義詞 】publishing house, publishing concern

purchase　v.　買, 購買

【同義詞】buy, shop

qualify　v.　使具有資格, 使合格

【同義詞】supply, provide for, outfit, equip

quality　n.　質, 質量

【同義詞】nature, kind, characteristic, constitution

quantity　n.　量

Track 71

【同義詞】amount, number, sum, measure

question　v.　詢問

【同義詞】inquire, ask, query, demand survey

questionnaire　　n.　問卷；（意見）調查表

【同義詞 】survey

quit　　v.　離開；退出

【同義詞 】stop, leave, cease, discontinue

quota　　n.　配額；定額；限額

【同義詞 】ratio, share, proportion, percentage

raise　　v.　舉起，抬起

【同義詞 】lift, increase, elevate, hoist

range　　n.　排，行；一系列

【同義詞 】limit, extent, distance, reach

rank　n.　等級；地位，身分

【同義詞】grade, class, position, rate

rapid　a.　快的，迅速的；動作快的

【同義詞】quick, swift, fast, speedy

react　v.　作出反應，反應

【同義詞】respond, answer

realize　v.　領悟，了解，認識到　

【同義詞】understand, grasp, conceive, comprehend

reasonable　a.　通情達理的，講道理的

【同義詞】sensible, fair, logical, just

rebuild　v.　重建；改建；重新組裝

【同義詞】reconstruct, remodel

recession　　n.　後退；衰退期

【同義詞 】recession, slump

recognize　　v.　認出，識別；認識

【同義詞 】acknowledge, see, behold, know

recruit　　v.　徵募(新兵)；吸收(新成員)

【同義詞 】enlist, draft, muster, enroll

reflect　　v.　反射；照出，映出

【同義詞 】mirror, send back, think, ponder

regard　　v.　注重，注意；考慮；關心

【同義詞 】consider, judge, think of

region　　n.　地區，地帶；行政區域

【同義詞 】place, space, area, location

release   v.   釋放, 解放

【同義詞】free, fire, relieve, dismiss

religious   a.   宗教的, 宗教上的

【同義詞】pious, devout, reverent, faithful

remain   v.   剩下, 餘留

【同義詞】continue, endure, persist, stay

replace   v.   把...放回(原處)

【同義詞】succeed, supply, come after, substitute for

representative   n.   典型, 代理人

Track
73

【同義詞】substitute, agent, lawyer, spokesman

require   v.   需要

【同義詞】need, necessitate, want, demand

resident　　n.　居民, 定居者; 僑民

【同義詞】inhabitant, habitant, occupant, denizen

resource　　n.　資源; 物力, 財力

【同義詞】natural wealth, property, goods

responsible　　a.　需負責任的, 承擔責任的

【同義詞】accountable, answerable, liable, trustworthy

result　　n.　結果, 成果

【同義詞】consequence, end, effect, outcome

resume　　n.　摘要, 履歷表

【同義詞】summary, curriculum vitae

retire　　v.　退休; 退役

【同義詞】resign, quit, vacate, relinquish

review v. 再檢查, 重新探討; 復審

【同義詞】study, remember, recall, learn

risk n. 危險, 風險

【同義詞】chance, hazard, gamble, venture

rule v. 規定; 統治, 管轄

【同義詞】govern, control, reign, dominate

Track
74

sacrifice v. 犧牲

【同義詞】relinquish, release, surrender, yield

script n. 筆跡; 劇本

【同義詞】writing, penmanship

security　n.　安全，安全感

【同義詞】safety, secureness, surety, safeness

segment　n.　部分；部門；切片，斷片

【同義詞】division, section, part, portion

sense　v.　感覺到；了解，領會

【同義詞】feel, perceive, understand, realize

sensitive　a.　敏感的；易受傷害的

【同義詞】impressionable, susceptible, receptive, susceptive

separate　v.　分隔；分割；使分離；使分散

【同義詞】divide, part, segregate, sort

serve　v.　為...服務；為...服役

【同義詞】supply, furnish, deliver, present

service　　n.　服務；效勞；幫助

【同義詞】assistance, help, aid, good turn

settle　　v.　安放；安頓；安排；料理

【同義詞】determine, decide, resolve, fix

share　　v.　一份；(分擔的)一部分

【同義詞】divide, proportion, apportion, distribute

ship　　v.　用船運；裝運；郵寄

【同義詞】transport, send, dispatch, haul

shoot　　v.　發射，放射

【同義詞】fire, discharge

shrink　　v.　收縮，縮短，皺縮

【同義詞】shrivel, wither, dwindle, become smaller

sign　n.　記號；招牌；手勢；徵兆

【同義詞】symbol, gesture, signal, symptom

similar　a.　相像的, 相仿的, 類似的

【同義詞】alike, like, resembling, same

site　n.　地點, 場所

【同義詞】place, location, position, situation

skill　n.　(專門)技術；技能, 技藝

【同義詞】ability, talent, gift, competence

solution　n.　解答；解決(辦法)；解釋

【同義詞】explanation, answer, resolution, finding

spread　v.　使伸展, 使延伸

【同義詞】unfold, extend, sprawl, stretch out

stable　a.　穩定的, 牢固的; 平穩的

【同義詞】steady, firm, unchanging, steadfast

staff　n.　（全體）職員,（全體）工作人員

【同義詞】group, committee, personnel, crew

stage　v.　上演; 發動

【同義詞】arrange, dramatize, present, produce

standard　n.　標準, 水準; 規格; 規範

【同義詞】model, rule, pattern, criterion

statement　n.　陳述, 說明

【同義詞】account, report, announcement, proclamation

status　n.　地位, 身分

Track
76

【同義詞】standing, position, station, class

steal　v.　偷，竊取

【同義詞】rob, take, thieve, pilfer

stock　v.　貯存；(知識等的)蓄積

【同義詞】keep, collect, accumulate, amass

strategy　n.　戰略；策略

【同義詞】planning, management, tactics, manipulation

strength　n.　力, 力量, 力氣；實力；效力

【同義詞】power, energy, force, vigor

struggle　v.　奮鬥；鬥爭

【同義詞】endeavor, strive, attempt, try

substitute　v.　代替

【同義詞】replace, change, exchange, switch

suggest　v.　建議, 提議

【同義詞】hint, imply, adumbrate, insinuate

supervise　v.　監督; 管理; 指導

【同義詞】direct, oversee, govern, regulate

support　v.　支撐, 支托, 扶持

【同義詞】help, aid, bolster, sustain

suppose　v.　猜想, 以為

【同義詞】believe, think, imagine, consider

surplus　n.　過剩; 剩餘物; 剩餘額

【同義詞】excess, extra, superfluous, remaining

survey　v.　俯視, 眺望, 環視

【同義詞】examine, view, scrutinize, review

system　n.　體系；系統

【同義詞】plan, scheme, method, design

talent　n.　天才，天資

【同義詞】ability, skill, gift, endowment

target　n.　靶子；目標，指標

【同義詞】object, goal, aim, end

task　n.　任務；工作；作業

【同義詞】work, duty, job, chore

tax　n.　稅；稅金

【同義詞】assessment, duty, imposition, impost, levy

technical　n.　工藝的；技術的；科技的

【同義詞 】specialized

tendency　n.　傾向；潮流；趨勢

【同義詞 】inclination, leaning, bent, proneness, propensity

term　n.　期，期限

【同義詞 】period, time, duration, condition

threat　n.　威脅，恐嚇

【同義詞 】warning, intimidation, caution

title　n.　標題，書名；頭銜，稱號

【同義詞 】tag, caption, designation, headline, denomination, denotation, designation

total　a.　總計的，總括的，全體的

【同義詞 】whole, entire, complete

tough   a.   堅韌的，牢固的，折不斷的

【同義詞 】hardy, strong, firm, sturdy

track   n.   行蹤；軌道；足跡

【同義詞 】line, railroad track, railway, way

train   v.   訓練，培養

【同義詞 】teach, rear, direct, drill

transaction   n.   辦理，處置，執行

【同義詞 】deal, trade, sale

trick   v.   哄騙，戲弄

【同義詞 】deceive, cheat, hoax, dupe

typical   a.   典型的，有代表性的

【同義詞 】representative, symbolic, characteristic, distinctive

ultimate a. 最後的，最終的

【同義詞】last, final, terminal, conclusive

unfortunately a. 不幸地

【同義詞】unluckily

urge v. 催促；力勸；激勵；慫恿

【同義詞】push, force, drive, plead

Track

79

vacant a. 空的；空白的

【同義詞】unoccupied, empty, void, barren

valid　a.　有根據的；確鑿的；令人信服的

【同義詞】sound, true, good, effective

value　n.　重要性，益處

【同義詞】worth, excellence, usefulness, importance

verbal　a.　言辭上的；言語的，字句的

【同義詞】oral, spoken, uttered, said

view　v.　觀看，考慮

【同義詞】see, sight, behold, observe

violate　v.　違犯；違背，違反

【同義詞】break, trespass, infringe

volunteer　v.　志願參加，自願提供

【同義詞】offer, come forward

vote   n.   選舉, 投票, 表決

【同義詞】ballot, choice, voice, poll

wage   n.   薪水；報酬

【同義詞】pay, payment, salary, remuneration

warn   v.   警告；告誡；提醒

【同義詞】inform, notify, caution, forebode

waste   v.   浪費；濫用；未充分利用

【同義詞】spend, squander, consume, exhaust

weaken   v.   削弱，減弱；減少

【同義詞】make less powerful

wealthy　a.　富的；富裕的；豐富的

【同義詞 】rich, affluent, prosperous, moneyed

weigh　v.　稱……的重量，掂估……的份量

【同義詞 】measure, gauge, assess, estimate

welfare　n.　福利；幸福；健康安樂

【同義詞 】good, benefit, interest, advantage

widespread　a.　分佈(或散佈)廣的；普遍的, 廣泛的

【同義詞 】expansive, extensive, far-reaching, wide

wisdom　n.　智慧，才智，明智

【同義詞 】insight, sense, sagacity, judiciousness

withdraw　v.　抽回；拉開；移開

【同義詞 】retreat, recede, retire, quit

witness v. 目擊；作證

【同義詞】testify, vouch, swear, see

workshop n. 工作場；工作坊

【同義詞】shop, workroom, atelier, loft

worldwide a. &adv. 遍及全球

【同義詞】around the world

worthwhile a. 值得花費時間(或金錢)的，值得做的

【同義詞】worth the time or effort

yield v. 出產；結出(果實)；產生(效果，收益等)

【同義詞】produce, give, grant, bear

youngster　　n.　小孩

【同義詞】child, minor, youth, kid

youth　　n.　青春時代, 青少年時期

【同義詞】childhood, early life, salad days, boyhood

yuppie　　n.　雅痞

【同義詞】young urban professionals

zone　　n.　地帶；地區

【同義詞】region, area, territory, place

永續圖書
線上購物網

www.foreverbooks.com.tw

◆　加入會員即享活動及會員折扣。

◆　每月均有優惠活動，期期不同。

◆　新加入會員三天內訂購書籍不限本數金額，

　　即贈送精選書籍一本。（依網站標示為主）

專業圖書發行、書局經銷、圖書出版

永續圖書總代理：

五觀藝術出版社、培育文化、棋茵出版社、犬拓文化、讀
品文化、雅典文化、知音人文化、手藝家出版社、璞申文
化、智學堂文化、語言鳥文化

活動期內，永續圖書將保留變更或終止該活動之權利及最終決定權。

國家圖書館出版品預行編目資料

史上最強GEPT Pro 企業英檢一本就夠 / 張文娟 著.
-- 初版. -- 新北市：雅典文化, 民103.09
面； 公分. -- (英語工具書；06)
ISBN 978-986-5753-19-1(平裝附光碟片)
1. 英語 2. 讀本

805.1892　　　　　　　　　103013998

英語工具書系列　06

史上最強GEPT Pro 企業英檢一本就夠

作者／張文娟
責編／張文娟
美術編輯／林子凌
封面設計／蕭若辰

法律顧問：方圓法律事務所／涂成樞律師

總經銷：永續圖書有限公司
永續圖書線上購物網
www.foreverbooks.com.tw

CVS代理／美璟文化有限公司
TEL：（02）2723-9968
FAX：（02）2723-9668

出版日／2014年09月

雅典文化

出版社

22103　新北市汐止區大同路三段194號9樓之1
TEL　（02）8647-3663
FAX　（02）8647-3660

史上最強GEPT Pro 企業英檢一本就夠

雅致風靡　典藏文化

親愛的顧客您好，感謝您購買這本書。

為了提供您更好的服務品質，煩請填寫下列回函資料，您的支持是我們最大的動力。

您可以選擇傳真、掃描或用本公司準備的免郵回函寄回，謝謝。

姓名：	性別：　□男　　□女
出生日期：　年　　月　　日	電話：
學歷：	職業：　□男　　□女
E-mail：	
地址：□□□	
從何得知本書消息：□逛書店 □朋友推薦 □DM廣告 □網路雜誌	
購買本書動機：□封面 □書名 □排版 □內容 □價格便宜	
你對本書的意見： 內容：□滿意□尚可□待改進　　編輯：□滿意□尚可□待改進 封面：□滿意□尚可□待改進　　定價：□滿意□尚可□待改進	
其他建議：	

總經銷：永續圖書有限公司

永續圖書線上購物網
www.foreverbooks.com.tw

您可以使用以下方式將回函寄回。

您的回覆，是我們進步的最大動力，謝謝。

① 使用本公司準備的免郵回函寄回。

② 傳真電話：（02）8647-3660

③ 掃描圖檔寄到電子信箱：

　　yungjiuh@ms45.hinet.net

沿此線對折後寄回，謝謝。

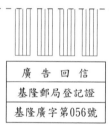

廣　告　回　信
基隆郵局登記證
基隆廣字第056號

2　2　1　-　0　3

 雅典文化事業有限公司　收

新北市汐止區大同路三段194號9樓之1

雅致風靡　　典藏文化

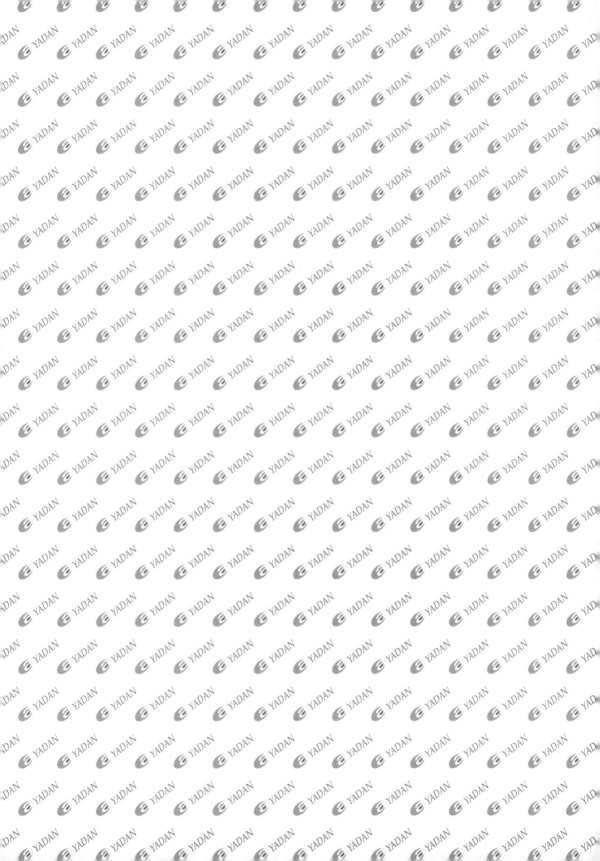